Every Frat Boy Wants It

Every Frat Boy Wants It

Todd Gregory

KENSINGTON BOOKS
www.kensingtonbooks.com

KENSINGTON BOOKS are published by

Kensington Publishing Corp.
850 Third Avenue
New York, NY 10022

All Kensington titles, imprints, and distributed lines are available at special quantity discounts for bulk purchases for sales promotion, premiums, fund-raising, educational, or institutional use.

Special book excerpts or customized printings can also be created to fit specific needs. For details, write or phone the office of the Kensington Special Sales Manager: Attn. Special Sales Department. Kensington Publishing Corp., 850 Third Avenue, New York, NY 10022. Phone: 1-800-221-2647.

Kensington and the K logo Reg. U.S. Pat. & TM Off.

ISBN-13: 978-0-7582-1719-6
ISBN-10: 0-7582-1719-6

First Printing: December 2007
10 9 8 7 6 5 4 3 2 1

Printed in the United States of America

This is for my editor
John Scognamiglio.
And for
Alex, Andy, Marc, Steve, and Stuart:
What happens in Vegas stays in Vegas.

PART ONE

SUMMER

Chapter 1

As I walk into the locker room of my high school to get my backpack, I'm aware of the sound of the shower running. Even before I walk around the corner that will reveal the rows of black lockers and the communal shower area just beyond, I can smell that pungent smell of sweat, dirty clothes, and sour jocks. I would never admit it to anyone, but I love that smell. Especially when it's warm outside—the smell seems riper, more vital, more alive. For me, it is the smell of athletic boys, the smell of their faded and dirty jockstraps. At night, when I lie in my bed alone jacking off in the quiet darkness, I close my eyes and I try to remember it. I imagine myself in that locker room after practice, the room alive with the sound of laughter and snapping towels, of boys running around in their jocks and giving each other bullshit as they brag about what girls they've fucked and how big their dicks are. I try to remember, as I lie there in my bed, the exact shape of their hard white asses, whose jockstrap is twisted just above the start of the curve, and below the muscled tan of their backs. It's the locker room where I first saw another boy naked, after all—the only place where it's acceptable to see other boys in various states of undress. The locker room always haunts my fantasies and my dreams.

And now, as I reach the corner, I hesitate. Who could still be showering at this time? Everyone else has left; baseball practice is long over, and I'd be in my car heading home myself if I hadn't forgotten my bag and I didn't have that damned History test tomorrow. Could it be Coach Wilson? I shudder at the thought. I certainly hoped it wasn't him. He was a nice man, but Coach Wilson was about a hundred years old and had a big old belly that made him look like he'd swallowed every single basketball in the equipment room. I take a deep breath and walk around the corner.

Maybe it was—um, no, that was too much to hope for. *Just get your bag and go.*

The locker room is filled with steam from the hot water in the shower. Wisps dance around the overhead lights, and it is so thick I can barely see the floor and make out the row of black painted metal lockers. Yet, through the steam, I can barely see a tanned form with his back turned to me, his head under the water spigot, hot water pouring down over his muscled back and over the perfectly round, hard whiteness of a mouth-wateringly beautiful ass. I catch my breath as I stare, knowing that I shouldn't—the right thing to do is call out a "hello," pretend not to look, get what I need, and get the hell out of there. But I am utterly transfixed by the sheer beauty of what I am seeing. I bite down on my lower lip, aware that my dick is getting hard in my pants as I watch. I can't tear myself away—I don't *want* to turn and go or stop staring, the body is too perfect. And with the wetness cascading down over it, the glistening flow of the water emphasizing every defined muscle in the lovely male form that has haunted my dreams and my fantasies ever since I transferred here my junior year and started going to this small rural high school. *Go, hurry, before he turns around and catches you watching—what are you going to say? Um, sorry, I was staring at your ass?*

But still I keep standing there, continuing to run the risk he'll catch me, every second passing making it more likely. How long can he stand there like that without moving?

But still—

How many times have I fantasized about him while pulling on my soapy dick in the shower at home? Or while lying in my bed after everyone else in the house has gone to sleep? Kneeling on the bathroom floor with the door locked behind me? How many times have I snuck glances over at him in the locker room after football practice, as he peeled off his pads and stood there in his jock turned grey from sweat? How many sidelong looks have I taken at his body as he stood under the shower, hoping that no one else noticed me looking at his crotch, the wet pubic hair, the curve of his balls, the length of his soft cock?

How many times have I sat next to him in the darkness of a movie theater, our knees almost touching as we scarf down popcorn and slurp sodas, hoping against hope our knees might brush against each other, or his hand might come down over mine on the armrest and squeeze gently? How many times have I hoped that he might want me too, that one night as we sat on a country road on the hood of a car sharing a six-pack of beer he might confess he desired me as much as I did him?

I've been in love with him almost from the first moment I saw him.

Just as I open my mouth to say something and let him know I'm there, he turns around and sees me.

"Jeff!" Kevin's handsome face breaks into a smile, and I almost melt right there. I don't think I have ever seen a boy anywhere as handsome as he is—and what makes him even handsomer is he has absolutely no idea the effect he has on people. Every girl at Southern Heights High School has had a crush on him at one time or another. He has the most amazing even, white teeth, his eyes are a deep shade of blue, and on top of his head is the thickest curly dark blond hair. When he smiles, his dimples carve deep grooves into the sides of his cheeks. Surely no other boy in history was as effortlessly beautiful as my best friend, Kevin Hansen.

"Hey, Kev." I force a smile on my face and try to keep my voice even. "Forgot my backpack." I focus on keeping my eyes on his face and resisting the urge to glance down. His body is also fantasy material. He's been lifting weights since junior high, and there's no fat anywhere on his body. His stomach is flat, hard and defined. And he has two brown quarter-shaped nipples that balance on his big hairless chest. His thickly muscled legs are covered with soft downy white hairs that are almost invisible unless they catch the light and flash gold.

"Oh." He glances down. I can't help myself, I look down as well, and I swallow hard. I can hear my heart pounding in my chest. He is soaping his crotch, and his hard-on is everything I could have dreamed of—thick and long. He looks back over at me. He smiles again, a little more shyly this time. "Wasn't expecting anyone, obviously." His cheeks color a little bit.

"Yeah, well." I feel myself turning red. My mouth is suddenly dry. I gulp. *Don't look at it, Jeff, look away and just grab your bag and get away from here before you do or say something stupid.*

"Looks like you've got one too, bro," he says teasingly, pointing with his soapy hand at my own crotch, where my traitorous erection is outlined against the denim. He rinses the soap off and steps out of the shower area and stands, his legs spread apart, not even ten yards away from me. Naked, dripping wet and erect, with his hands on his hips, posed like some kind of Greek god, almost as if he's daring me to look, he laughs. "What do you say, Jeff?"

"Um, about what?" I reply, feeling like the lamest idiot on the planet. *Surely he can't mean—no, life doesn't work like that, dreams and fantasies about other boys don't come true, and Kevin's not that way, you're the only freak who dreams about other guys and sucking their dicks, who steals glances in the locker room.*

"Remember all those wrestling matches we've had?" he goes on in a low voice, like I haven't said a word.

"Um, yeah." Like I could ever forget them? Every time I'd spent the night at his house, or he'd stayed at mine, we'd had a wrestling match in our underwear. We pretended like we were WWE superstars, but not doing any of the crazier stuff—wrestling around like boys. We talked trash to each other before, after, and during. Kevin, being bigger and stronger, almost always won. I didn't care so much about winning—although he seemed to enjoy it when he won. He'd jump up and flex his arms, talk about what a stud he was, and all that kind of stuff.

Of course, I was never really trying to win. I was more interested in the closeness of our sweating bodies, the way his muscles felt against mine, the way he smelled, while at the same time hoping against hope he'd never notice that my

cock was hard. I sometimes wondered if his was as well—
but never dared to look. I certainly never dared to actually
touch him there. Even though I knew deep down Kevin
and I would never be together, I liked being around him. I
didn't want to lose that. And those wrestling matches were
prime jack-off memories for me. Generally after one of
them I'd go straight into the bathroom and remember the
highlights as I jacked off—which didn't take long anyway. I
was so turned on by the wrestling it's a wonder I didn't
come during the match. There was one time he'd wrapped
his legs around my head and squeezed, my face going right
into his crotch. Even though it hurt, I hadn't wanted to give
up. I wanted my face to stay there all night. That was my favorite memory—but he'd never done that to me again.

I always wondered why.

"Those always turned me on." He puts his right hand on
his cock. "Man, I always wanted to suck your dick, bro."

Gulp. "Um, seriously?" I feel like a crushing dork. The
boy I love just told me he wants to suck my dick and
that's all I can think of to say? I can feel my face turning
redder, and my own dick is straining against the fly of my
jeans.

"Oh, yeah, man. I've always thought you were sexy, you
know." He grins and leans forward, and his lips press
against mine. Electricity rushes through my body; I can feel
a tingling all the way to the tips of my toes and fingers. My
lips part and his tongue enters my mouth, and I stroke the
bottom of it with my own. My hands come up and touch his
chest, my fingertips brushing against his nipples. I can feel
his entire body stiffen and a low moan begins in his throat.
I open my eyes as he pulls his head back from mine, and he
whispers, "I love you so much, Jeff—"

* * *

"Dude, class is over."

Startled, I jumped and opened my eyes, somehow managing to knock my notebook and pen onto the floor. "Fuck!" Embarrassed, I looked around. The classroom was empty, and the clock on the wall showed that class had been over for a few minutes.

"You were having one hell of a daydream, though." The voice continued, a note of amusement evident. As I slowly became more aware that I was, indeed, still seated at my desk, I turned to get a look at the guy talking to me. He was standing to my left in the aisle, a backpack slung over his left shoulder and expensive looking mirrored sunglasses covering his eyes. His hair was bluish black and gelled so it stood up in every which way. He was wearing a pale blue T-shirt that said *Stiff Competition Wrestling* on it, with the graphic of two guys in singlets on a mat in the center of the lettering. The shirt fit him tightly, and veins showed in his tanned forearms. He was wearing a matching pair of long shorts that stopped just below his knees, and a pair of leather sandals. His calves were also well-defined and covered in thick, black curly hair. His arms were crossed, and there was a huge smile on his handsome face. Dimples danced in his cheeks, and his lips were thick. There was a slight bluish black stubble under his nose. "Can't say as I blame you. Is there anything more boring in this life than Macro Economics?" He tilted his head to one side. "Maybe Micro Economics, or Biology, or pretty much any required class at this stupid school." He stuck his right hand out. "Blair Blanchard."

Uncomfortably aware of both my hard-on and how tight my jean shorts were, I stayed in my seat. "Um, Jeff Morgan." I shook his hand. His hand was dry, the grip firm, even though my hand was a lot bigger than his.

"Nice to meet ya, Jeff." As I stayed in my seat, he cocked his head to one side again. "Your next class in this room?"

"Um. No." I could feel my cheeks starting to turn red again. My cock was still hard. *I am never wearing tight shorts in public again,* I decided.

He knelt down and handed me my notebook and my pen. "Then someone is going to be needing your seat, don't you think?"

"Um, yeah. I guess."

He threw his head back and laughed. "So, you had an erotic daydream and got a big ol' boner, Jeff. It's no big deal. I read somewhere that the wind can give guys our age a hard-on if it blows on us just right—and I think that's true. Besides, probably half the guys walking around on campus right now have one. Get over it." He slapped me on the shoulder. "Come on, bud, if you don't have another class, I'll buy you a soda at the Pit."

"Okay." I adjusted myself a bit before standing up and slipping my notebook and pen into my backpack. My mind was spinning. No one before in my life had ever so casually talked about anyone else's boner before—at least not in front of me, at least not without referencing slipping it to a girl—you know, the typical locker room I'm-such-a-stud bullshit. All through high school I'd wondered if my team-mates really were getting as much action as they claimed when they were undressed. As I stood up, he walked up the aisle and I couldn't help but stare at his ass. The shorts rode low on his hips, and there was a line of tanned skin where the T-shirt rode up on his back. His ass, like Kevin's, was round and hard, but his was more compact. He was a lot more slender and lean than Kevin, who had a football player's thick body. Blair looked more like one of those guys who maybe ran a middle distance on the track team. Or maybe a swimmer—he did have pretty broad shoulders for his size. I followed him out. *Polk, California*, I thought, *sure is a long way from Kewanee, Kansas*.

Kewanee was where I'd graduated from high school barely a month earlier.

I'd been born and raised in Newton, Kansas, where my father worked for the Great Plains Pacific railroad as an engineer. No, he didn't drive trains; he was a structural engineer, building bridges and buildings. I was an only child, and after my sophomore year at Newton High my father was transferred to Emporia. Mom and Dad decided to buy a house in the nearby town of Kewanee because it was cheaper, not realizing I was going to have to go to a small, consolidated rural high school called Southern Heights High rather than Emporia High until it was too late. They'd been very apologetic, and with good reason it turned out. Southern Heights was tiny; one hundred and eighty students drawn from seven small towns scattered throughout the southern part of the county. All the kids there had been going to school together since they started school; they didn't get many new kids and I stood out. But I was also lucky—as a football player, I had instant status in the school, especially since I'd lettered at the much bigger Newton High. I was a fullback, and became instant friends with Kevin Hansen, the starting halfback. My two years at Southern Heights wound up being pretty cool—I made a lot of friends, got invited to parties, and there was always a girl who had a crush on me. It would have been perfect if not for the fact that I was madly in love with my best friend. It was so weird. At Newton High there were guys I'd get a crush on for a while, but nothing like the way I felt about Kevin.

And Kevin was a really cool guy. Even if I hadn't fallen in love with him, I think we'd have been good friends anyway. We had the same sense of humor, we took the same classes, we liked the same kind of movies. We'd made a lot of plans together—we were both going to go to Kansas State, be roommates in the dorm, maybe join the same fraternity.

I was never sure if Kevin's feelings for me went deeper than friendship, and was too much of a coward to ever make the first move on him. But he never really seemed that interested in the girls he dated, so I always wondered if he was carrying the same torch I was, and like me, was too afraid to try anything.

When I found out we were moving away, I considered trying something our last night together, but instead we just went to a movie and hung out.

"I'm gonna miss you, bro," Kevin said as he hugged me good-bye. "You make sure you write, okay?"

The Pit was in the student union at California State University-Polk, a school I'd never even heard of six months before when my father came home to announce that he'd been transferred yet again. It was a big promotion for him, and when my parents sat me down to tell me the news, I saw my four years at Kansas State going up in smoke.

"It's just too far, son," my father had said gently. "And CSU-Polk is a really good school. We know it's going to be hard on you, but look at it as a big adventure."

I'd just nodded, even though I was more than a little pissed off.

Yeah, some adventure. Thousands of miles away from my

friends, away from the only state I'd ever known, to a thriving city in the middle of the San Joaquin Valley.

It was like moving to another planet.

And I was lonely.

The summer session was two weeks along, and I hadn't met anyone, made any friends.

I hated Polk and wanted to go home.

I followed Blair into the Pit, which was crowded with students, and got myself a bottle of Coke from the cooler. He paid, and we found a booth in a secluded corner of the big room. "So, Jeff, what brings you to See As You Pee?"

I had just taken a drink of my Coke and started laughing, so it came out as a snort and Coke went up my nose. I started gagging and coughing, and grabbed a napkin out of the dispenser to blow my nose. I wiped at my eyes. "Jesus!"

"Never heard that before?" He had a bemused expression on his face. "This must be your first semester here."

"Yeah, yeah it is." I finally had it under control and grinned back at him. "I'd never even heard of this school a year ago."

He nodded. "Not many people outside of the state have. So, where are you from?"

"Kansas."

"Ah, the land of Dorothy." The smile never faltered. "And what's your major?"

"English."

"And what dorm?"

I looked down at my Coke. "I live with my parents."

"You live in Polk?" His eyebrows arched up over the sunglasses. "I didn't think anyone actually lived here."

"My dad got transferred." I shrugged. "I'd planned on going to Kansas State, but with the transfer..." I let my voice trail off. No sense in pouring out my troubles to a total stranger.

"So you wound up here." He nodded, "Made any friends?"

I shook my head.

His smile came back. "Well, now you have." He stuck his hand out again. "I'm Blair, and I'm your new best friend."

I stared at his hand for a minute, then took it. "Cool."

"Come on. You don't have any more classes today?"

"No, but—" I hesitated. "I need to go out and apply for a job."

He waved his hand. "Plenty of time for that. You've just made a new best friend, and we need to celebrate." He jumped up, threw his backpack over his shoulder, and put both hands on his hips. "You coming, new best friend?"

I considered for a second. Mom and Dad were paying for my tuition and books, and giving me a place to live—but had made it clear any money I needed beyond that, I'd have to earn myself. I'd worked at the Emporia McDonalds part-time my entire senior year, and the money I'd saved from that was running out. I had put applications in at a couple of department stores, but was resisting fast food. I'd liked working at McDonalds, primarily because Kevin had worked there too—but without him, I didn't really want to get all sweaty and greasy every time I went to work again. Surely there had to be other places that would hire me? But I hadn't really tried too hard to find a job, and I had a feeling Mom and Dad would be a little more sympathetic than they'd said. They hadn't really pushed it much since we'd gotten here. I looked up at my new best friend and grinned. "Sure, what did you have in mind?"

"Let's go to my fraternity house and hang out; you can meet some of the guys." He raised the sunglasses again and winked. "Maybe you could join up." He laughed, and added in a serious voice, "It's like having eighty best friends, you know. Best cure for loneliness in the world." He dropped the sunglasses back down. "Although there are times when I really miss being lonely."

Chapter 2

Blair's car was parked in the lot behind the library. I whistled when we got to it. It was a silver Lexus convertible, and still had that new car smell on the inside when I got in. My own car used to be my parents', and they'd just passed it on to me when they bought a new one when I turned sixteen. It was an eighteen year old Oldsmobile Delta Royale 88, with a navy blue paint job at one time, but apparently the paint had been defective so it kind of looked like it had leprosy. My parents had gotten it as a wedding present from my grandparents, and they'd babied it like you wouldn't believe—oil change every three thousand miles, regular tune-ups, and so on. The end result was despite the fact it looked like it belonged up on blocks in a field somewhere, it ran like it was brand new. I called it the Flying Couch, because that's what the ride felt like—like you were driving a couch down the road. I'd never really cared much about how the car looked—I was just grateful that I had one. Most of my classmates at Southern Heights either had to buy their own cars, rebuild one, or do without.

But my car was nothing compared to Blair's Lexus. As

soon as he had the top down, he plugged his iPod into the stereo and the car filled with the sound of a techno dance mix at top volume. He dug around in his backpack and pulled out a rumpled pack of Marlboro Lights. He offered the pack to me and I shook my head. "Nasty habit," he said as he shook one out for himself. "I wish I'd never started."

"When did you start?" I shouted over the woman who was wailing through the speakers. I started bopping my head around to the beat. It was a great song.

"When I was twelve," he shouted back, shoving the car into reverse and screeching out of the parking spot. He stopped the car with a lurch and grinned over at me. "Deborah Cox is awesome, isn't she? I fucking love her." He lit the cigarette and slammed the car into drive and we shot off with another squeal of burning rubber.

"Yeah." I shouted back as he veered out of the parking lot and started driving about thirty miles above the speed limit along the road that bordered the back of the campus. An orange grove stretched for miles in the distance on the other side of the road, and I found myself clutching the dashboard.

A light changed and he slammed on the brakes, throwing me forward. He turned the volume down, and gave me that grin again. "Sorry. I like speed."

"It's okay," I replied weakly. I uncapped my Coke bottle and took a long swig, listening to my heart thumping in my ears. "I might have to change my underwear at some point, but it's okay."

"Good one!" He threw his head back and laughed. "Really. I'm sorry. I forget sometimes to be a little more respectful when other people are in the car. When I'm by myself heading home, I really open her up going down the grapevine.

There's nothing like driving fast in a car that knows how to handle it." He went on, "My dad has a Aston Martin, you know, like James Bond? Sometimes he lets me drive it out to our place in Palm Springs. That baby can fly."

The light changed, and he drove through the intersection at a normal, law-abiding speed, for which I was grateful. He drove down a few more blocks, and then turned left, driving alongside the parking lot of the football stadium. About halfway down the block he turned right into a short street that ended in a cul-de-sac. The street was lined with parking lots behind large buildings. The parking lots were mostly empty; the ones on the right completely vacant. "That side," he gestured to the right, "is the back side of sorority row. Delta Gamma on the corner, then Kappa Alpha Theta, and then Alpha Xi Delta. This side"—he gestured to the left— "is the backside of the fraternities. Lambda Chi Alpha, Sigma Alpha Epsilon, and here . . ." He headed to the very end of the cul-de-sac and drove into the last parking lot to the left. There were several cars in the lot, and at the end a huge pole with a basketball backboard and hoop split the asphalt into two sections. He drove right up to the building and pulled into a spot. He shut the car off and grinned at me. "Welcome to Beta Kappa."

I got out of the car, resisting the urge to kiss the ground, and looked at the building. It was shaped in an L, around a yard with two massive trees. It was painted white with brown trim. A huge hammock was hanging between the massive tree trunks, and the lawn looked a little spotty in places. The lower end of the L was only half the height of the other side, with a wall almost completely of glass from which curtains hung. A huge red metal BK hung beside the door to the glass wall. A sidewalk ran alongside the building to this door, and bushes grew up beside it to shield the windows on that floor. In the two-story part of the building, which I was facing, was another door and a huge window on the second floor directly above. A guy was standing in that window, a cigarette in one hand, a Super Big Gulp in the other, just staring out.

Blair waved at him. "That's Jerry Pollard," he said when the guy inclined his hand in a slight wave back. "He loves to stare out the window all day." He grinned at me. "He's a little odd, but okay for the most part. But when he gets really drunk, he's weepy." He shuddered. "Don't ever get cornered by him—it's almost impossible to get away."

"Um, okay," I replied, looking up at him. He was wearing a baggy sweatshirt and jeans, with a CSUP baseball cap pulled down low on his forehead. "Any particular reason?"

"Nah. I think he just gets depressed when he drinks."

"No, I mean why he stands in the window all the time."

Blair laughed. "I don't know. I've never asked. Maybe I should sometime." He headed for the doorway. "Come on."

I followed him into a hallway with a staircase directly to the right. It was gloomy and hot in the hallway, almost stiflingly so. The whole place smelled like old dirty gym socks. The hallway was painted white, and there was an all-weather carpet down on the floor. The doors were all painted brown, with small gold numbers mounted on them over peepholes. At the end of the hallway I could see a green chalkboard and mailboxes mounted on the wall. I took a deep breath. I could feel sweat forming under my arms and along my scalp, and I was considering pulling off my shirt when I was about halfway down the hall. Without warning, two saloon doors to my right suddenly swung open, almost hitting me. I jumped back, lost my balance, and fell back into the opposite wall.

"Dude! Are you okay? Man, I am so sorry."

"Um, yeah." I picked myself up off the floor and looked up at a handsome guy who had to be at least six four. He had bright blue eyes and curly brown hair, and he was grinning down at me.

He was also stark naked.

"Armagh, why don't you watch where you're going?" Blair snapped, walking back to us. "You could have hurt a prospective! Are you all right, Jeff?"

"Dude, I said I'm sorry." He stuck out a huge right hand. "Rory Armagh."

"Um, Jeff Morgan." His hand closed around mine as I tried not to stare at him. His body was absolutely amazing. Broad, thick shoulders, huge chest, arms, flat stomach, a sprinkling of hair down the center of his chest to his—I definitely looked away after a quick glance.

He was HUGE.

"Nice to meet you, man." He clapped a hand on my shoulder.

"Rory's on the water polo team and an alternate to the national team." Blair said from somewhere to my left. "And not exactly the sharpest knife in the drawer, if you catch my drift."

"Ah, fuck you, Blair," Rory said good-naturedly. "Seriously, man, you are okay, aren't you?" When I nodded, he winked at me. "Well, if you guys want to spark one later, let me know," Rory said, turning to walk down the hall. "I got some killer shit last night. You're gonna love it," he called back over his shoulder.

I bit my lower lip. *Doesn't he know the outside door is open and anyone outside can see him?* I wondered. *But then again, if I looked like that, I probably wouldn't care either.*

"You'll have to forgive Rory and don't judge the house by him," Blair said. "He's the only one who walks around naked. We're going to have to pass a new house rule about it, I think, when the fall semester starts again. Ah, well, I guess it's because he's done porn."

"What?" I couldn't have heard that right. "Did you say—"

"Yeah, he's done some porn. Come on, my room's right over here."

I turned back to stare after Rory's white hard ass as it disappeared into a room we'd already walked past. I shook my head. He certainly had the body for porn, I figured. I'd never really seen any porn, just heard about it. My parents had our Internet service blocked for that. But . . . yeah, I'd pay money to see Rory naked.

I turned back as Blair slipped a key into a door and walked inside. I walked down the rest of the hallway and stepped through the door.

The room was about the same size—maybe a little smaller—as my bedroom at my parents', but there was a lot more crammed into it. Up against one wall, there was a dresser and a desk with a laptop computer on it, and an iPod stereo system opposite a single bed directly across. A closet door hung open and I could see it was stuffed to overflowing with clothes. A window unit was humming and it was about thirty degrees cooler in the room than in the hallway. Blair opened a small refrigerator. "You want a beer?"

"Um, no." I'd never had a drink of anything in my life harder than a glass of champagne once at a wedding. A lot of the kids at both Newton and Southern Heights had drank, I just never had. I'd tasted a beer once at a party, but hadn't cared for the taste. I never could understand the other athletes at either school who drank and smoked—my parents always told me that you couldn't be an athlete and do either, and the coaches had always said the same thing.

"Okay." Blair shrugged, removing his sunglasses and putting them on his desk. I started looking at the posters on the walls. They were all movie posters: *Action Hero* and *Vietnam Rescue* starring Steve Blanchard on one wall—the ones on the facing wall were *Mary Queen of Scots* and *To the Lighthouse* starring Nicole Blair.

And then it clicked in my head.

I looked at one wall. "Blair," I said aloud, and then looked at the other. "Blanchard."

Blair grinned at me as he opened the bottom drawer of his dresser. "Brilliant deduction, Sherlock. You'd be amazed how many people never get it and I have to tell them." He rolled his eyes. "Shut and lock the door." I did. "Yup, Mom and Dad." He laughed. "I'm what they call a 'star baby', although they got divorced when I was little. I don't remember them ever being married to each other." He placed a large glass dragon and a baggie full of something on the desktop, and started filling a little silver bowl on the side of the dragon with pieces of something from the baggie. "Sit." He gestured at the bed, so I sat down there, shrugging off my backpack. He got up and placed a towel along the bottom of the door, then walked back and lit the bowl, inhaling deeply as it filled with smoke. He set it back down, sat there for a few seconds before blowing a huge aromatic stream of smoke at the ceiling.

"Your parents are Nicole Blair and Steve Blanchard." I couldn't quite wrap my head around it. "But they're *movie stars!*"

"Yeah, well, you're not in Kansas anymore, bud." He took another hit. "Movie stars are a dime a dozen out here. And Mom's not really a movie star, although she's won an Oscar, which is more than Dad can say," he said after exhaling another cloud.

"Wow." No one back at home would believe that I had a class with Steve Blanchard's son. My parents would freak, too. My parents were huge fans of Steve Blanchard. He was the only movie star whose movies they'd pay to see at the theater. And when they came out on video, they rented them. They were crazy about him. Frankly, I didn't think he could act and his movies all pretty much seemed the same to me, but he was a lot of fun to watch. He had an amazingly sculpted body, a beautiful face, and the deepest blue eyes—and in almost every movie he made at some point he was naked, covered in oil and tortured. Not that they ever showed his dick or anything, but his ass—his ass was almost as big a star as he was.

He offered me the dragon. "Oh, no thanks, I don't." I waved it off.

"Have you ever tried?" He looked at me. "Like I said, bro, you're not in Kansas anymore."

I hesitated. In one side of my head, I could hear my parents' endless lectures. *Smoking pot is just the start, once you try it you get hooked and if that drug is okay for you, and doesn't mess you up so bad, well, why not try cocaine and crystal meth and heroin or LSD and before you know it you're so badly hooked on something you can't stop, and you're destroying your body and your mind, and you're such a smart boy, Jeff, with such a brilliant future ahead of you. Don't be stupid.*

But on the other side, there was another voice, the one I'd heard before but always managed to suppress.

But your parents wouldn't love you, Jeff, if they knew what you were really like—that you liked boys instead of girls, that you dream of other boys, that the thought of kissing another boy is what gets you excited; kissing a girl doesn't do anything for you at all. What would your parents say about that? What would they say if you told them the truth? They'd throw you out, that's what they'd do. You've heard them talk about the "queers," and have they ever said anything that would make you think otherwise? They think queers are freaks, and you're a queer. You've tried to change that, you've gone out with girls, and it hasn't done you any good. You've gone to church and you've prayed, and it hasn't done you a damned bit of good. So why be good? You're bad, through and through, and they've always told you so. So what? Try it. Once won't kill you.

I looked at Blair.

I looked at the dragon.

I reached for it. "Um, what do I do?"

"Ah, I love corrupting the innocent." He grinned, and sat down next to me on the bed. "Well, you see this little hole? You put your thumb over that, okay?" I did as he told me. "Now put your mouth over the big hole here at the top." I did, smelling the water inside the glass, which was kind of nauseating. "Okay, when I light the lighter and put it against the pot, you start sucking in air, okay?"

I nodded.

He lit the lighter.

I started sucking.

"Now take your thumb off."

I did, and inhaled a huge rush of smoke.

And choked.

I started coughing, hard.

I couldn't stop. It felt like I was NEVER going to stop. I

coughed and gagged, then coughed some more. My throat burned, my eyes watered, and Blair handed me my Coke. "Take a drink," he ordered.

I swallowed, and that soothed the burning in my throat enough so the coughing stopped.

"My God." I finally managed to choke the words out before finishing the rest of my Coke. "That's horrible." But even as I said the words, I could feel a weird kind of numbness moving through my mind. I'd never felt anything like it before, and as I looked at Blair, I started to giggle. "Oh, wow." I said, and the words seemed to echo and bounce around inside my head. I looked over at the poster for *Mary Queen of Scots*, and the red velvet dress and pearls Nicole Blair was wearing seemed—somehow almost alive with vibrancy, it was almost as though she weren't a poster image but actually there, breathing.

"Have another hit, " Blair said from somewhere nearby, and I took the dragon in my hands again and obediently put my thumb and mouth in place.

This time I didn't cough at all, and I could feel my mind completely relaxing, and my entire body seemed to be floating somehow. I looked over at Blair, who was taking another hit.

He's beautiful, I told myself, *look at those eyes*.

Now that I knew who he was, I could see he had his father's eyes, his mother's bone structure and skin. I wanted to touch him, to kiss him.

He's even more beautiful than Kevin.

He put the dragon down, and he reached over and put his fingers on my face. "How you doing there, Jeffy?"

I smiled. "I'm good, it's all good." I giggled again. "Wow. This feels amazing."

Blair leaned in and kissed me.

My entire body responded. It was like an electric current was going through me, my entire body felt sensitized and my cock immediately got hard. His lips weren't like I'd imagined Kevin's to be. They were soft but firm, and he tasted slightly of smoke and Coke. As he kissed me, he slid across the surface of the bed until his leg was touching mine, and his arms went around me. I put mine around him and pulled him closer to me. It was everything I'd ever dreamed of, only better. He pushed against me a little bit, and I leaned back until I was on my back, and he rolled over on top of me. I put my arms around him, feeling the muscles in his back and he started grinding his crotch on top of mine.

He stopped kissing me and raised himself up on his elbows and looked into my eyes. "You doing okay there, Jeffy?"

I smiled at him. My head was still full of fog, but I knew I wanted him to keep going, I didn't want him to stop. "Uh-huh."

"Maybe we'd better stop." He got to his feet and smiled down at me. I could see the bulge in the front of his shorts.

"Why?" I sat up. "I don't want to stop."

"Have you ever done anything like this before?"

"Yes," I lied.

"With who?"

"Kevin, my best friend in Kansas."

He sat down in his desk chair and started reloading the bowl. He gave me a bemused look. "Really? And what did you and Kevin do with each other?"

"We, um, we sucked each other off."

He took a hit and put the dragon back down. He blew

the smoke out. "And how did Kevin taste? Did he come in your mouth?"

"He—" I hesitated.

"Don't lie to me, Jeffy. You're really bad at it." He gave me a smile as he lit another cigarette. "Look, you're cute as hell and that body"—he pursed his lips and whistled—"but the last thing I want is to take advantage of you when you're stoned." He flicked ash on the floor. "When they're fucked up, Jeffy, straight boys will do pretty much anything with anyone to get their rocks off. Afterward, they either pretend it never happened, or they hate the guy it happened with." He laughed bitterly. "Trust me on that, okay? And I do like you, Jeffy, and I want us to be friends. But I don't want you to wake up tomorrow thinking 'Man, that asshole Blair, he got me stoned and took advantage of me', or pretend you don't know me in class tomorrow."

"I wouldn't do that."

"Okay, sure you wouldn't." He shrugged. "We'll see."

"Dude—"

"Yeah." He stood up and stretched. "I'm hungry. You wanna order a pizza or something?"

"Sure," I said, my hard-on starting to go down. I smiled at him.

One day, Blair, one day . . .

Chapter 3

What happened between us that first afternoon didn't happen again, no matter how much I wanted it to.

I was afraid to bring it up, and Blair never did.

It was like it never happened in the first place; a figment of my imagination created by a pot-impaired brain. But in my heart I knew it had happened. I could still taste his lips, feel his arms around me, the feel of our crotches working against each other. He replaced Kevin in my fantasies until I couldn't even remember what Kevin looked like. One night, I tried to summon up Kevin's image, and wound up having to get my yearbook to get an idea. As I looked down at Kevin's senior picture, I shook my head. *Why were you so obsessed with him? He's nowhere near as cute as Blair—and Blair's a lot more fun to hang out with.*

We started spending a lot of time together. Every morning, he'd pick me up for class and we'd smoke a joint on the way to the campus. That made Macro Economics a lot more interesting, even though I spent most of my time daydreaming about Blair. Whenever I could, I would watch him and try to commit details to memory, so I could call them up later in my bed. I loved the way his shoulders tapered down to his waist. I loved how his torso was almost completely hairless—except for the wiry black hairs that led from his navel down to his waistband. I loved how he only wore Versace underwear, and only black. And my parents loved him—the allure of being the son of their favorite movie star was too much for them. As long as I was with Blair, I could stay out as late as I wanted, and Mom never mentioned me getting a job again. It wasn't like I needed money anyway—Blair always had money, and Blair always wanted to pay my way. It didn't matter if it was a movie, or popcorn for the movie, or the Carl's Jr. drive-through, or pizza—Blair always paid. I kept the same twenty in my wallet day after day, just in case I should ever need it.

But I never did. Blair would get mad if I even reached for my wallet, so eventually I stopped trying. "What's the point of having a rich father," he'd say, "if you can't treat people to something every once in a while?"

And spending a lot of time with him meant spending a lot of time at the Beta Kappa house. Blair didn't really like to go to movies, and we weren't old enough to go to bars anyway. "Besides, the only people we'd meet there are *locals*," he would say, forgetting that I was one, "and spend a lot of money on watered-down drinks. We can drink here a lot cheaper—and better." And, as he wisely pointed out, we couldn't exactly get stoned and drink beer at my house with my mother around. And so, I somehow moved from prospective pledge to guaranteed pledge—even though they couldn't officially offer me a bid until the fall semester started. It just seemed kind of natural that I'd join Beta Kappa. It was a lot of fun hanging around the house—even though I didn't get to see Rory Armagh coming out of the showers naked again. Every so often, for a change of pace, when I lay in my bed at night pulling on my dick, I tried to remember every detail of Rory's naked body. But even as I got closer and closer to shooting my load, Blair would push Rory out of my mind. And I loved watching Blair whenever we were together, and unlike with Kevin, I didn't care if he noticed. I wanted him to notice. I wanted him to know that whenever he decided it was okay, I was ready to be kissed again. I was ready to make love to him, hold him, suck his dick— even let him fuck me, if he wanted to. My entire world revolved around him, and while I did like the other brothers who were staying at Beta Kappa over the summer—mostly smoking pot and drinking every day—I just wanted to be with Blair.

I got aroused whenever he stretched, memorizing what his flat stomach looked like so I could remember later, or when he bent over to pick something up, as his shorts rode down and his shirt went up, giving me a tantalizing glimpse of his tan line and the crack of his beautiful ass.

I wanted him more than I'd ever dreamed of wanting Kevin.

The other brothers I met were pretty cool. I spent some time hanging out with Jerry Pollard, and found out that the reason he spent so much time looking out the upstairs window at the parking lots was it helped him to focus his creative energies. He wanted to be a writer—as did I—and he was very helpful by giving me the rundown on what classes to take and what classes to avoid in the English department. He was writing a fantasy novel, but no matter how many questions I asked he wouldn't tell me anything about it. "What are you writing?" he asked me finally to get the subject off his own book.

I took a hit out of his bong. It wasn't as smooth as Blair's dragon, but I thought it was cool that it was shaped like Gandalf from *Lord of the Rings*. Jerry's whole room was done in Tolkien. "Oh, I'm not ready to write anything yet," I replied, passing him the bong back and taking a swig out of my Bud Light. I was developing quite a taste for beer during my time spent at the Beta Kappa house. "I still have a lot to learn, I think."

He frowned at me. "That's just *dumb*, Jeff, and you're not a dumb guy. Young maybe, immature certainly, but not dumb." He took a hit.

"What do you mean?" I asked. Fortunately, I was pleasantly stoned, otherwise I would have probably gotten pissed at being called young and immature.

"Writers write," he said, waving Gandalf in front of my nose. "Even if it's crap. You should spend at least an hour or two each day writing—even if it's just a journal or a diary, or whatever. Even if it's just venting about something stupid that happened to you that day. It can be great therapy, you know. Writing is like anything else, Jeffy—the more you do it, the better you get at it. Practice, practice, practice."

Later, in Blair's room and on my fifth beer, I mentioned what Jerry had said, and Blair frowned at me. "You never told me you wanted to be a writer."

"You never asked." I reached for the dragon and the lighter.

"You should tell your best friend these things, you know. You want to write fiction or screenplays?" He handed me the bag of weed. "I think that's empty."

"Fiction. I want to write books." I loaded the bowl and took a hit. "I want to be a bestselling author whose books are turned into movies, whose books inspire people to be better people, and be rich and famous and well-respected, asked to speak at colleges . . ." I grinned, "That kind of thing." I shrugged. "I know, it seems silly, but that's what I dream of."

"Why do you think it's silly?" Blair demanded, standing up and walking over to the refrigerator. "You should have dreams—otherwise how are you going to know what you want?"

I dream about you all the time, I wanted to say, but instead I said, "My parents—" I hesitated. "My parents tell me I should get a degree in something useful, so I'll have something to fall back on if I don't make it as a writer." I probably wouldn't have admitted that if I hadn't been stoned. It hurt when my parents told me to major in business rather than creative writing. *Don't you believe in me?* I'd wanted to scream at them, but they were just being practical, and it was from love.

Or so I told myself every day.

"Parents. Blech." Blair knelt down in front of the refrigerator. "Well, then Jerry's right, you should be writing every day." Blair opened the refrigerator and got us both another beer. "You shouldn't be wasting all your time—not of course that time spent with me is time wasted."

"Lighten up, dude." I giggled. "What do you want to be when you grow up? You've never told me either."

"I want to be an actor." He glanced at his father's posters. "Not like him, but like *her.*" He walked over to his mother's images and stared up at them. "She's an actress, a true talent, not like Dad, who's just kind of good looking in a generic kind of way. Oh, don't get me wrong, he has charisma or whatever you want to call it—the kind of thing stars have—but Mom, she's got real talent." He looked back at me. "She can play anything, you know? She is amazing. She's not the prettiest actress out there, she's not the most charismatic, but there's just something about her . . . when she's on camera, you can't look away from her."

"I've never seen one of her movies," I admitted.

"Well, one of these days we'll have to have a Nicole Blair film festival." He replied with a grin. "Would you like that? We could watch *To the Lighthouse*—that's my favorite, even though she won the Oscar for *Mary Queen of Scots*, which is also a good one, but I think the romance she did with Burt Reynolds—that's her best performance, probably. I mean, she was convincing—and it can't be easy to convince people you're in love with *him*."

"Sure." I couldn't ever say no to Blair about anything. I wanted him to smile at me. I kept thinking, *If I could just please him, if I could just make him happy, maybe he would kiss me again.* There were times when I thought I should make the first move—maybe he was just waiting for me? At night, in my bed, after I had wiped my come off myself with a Kleenex and lay there staring at the ceiling, wondering if the day would ever come when he would want me again, I would decide to be more assertive—to grow some balls, to know what I wanted and go for it. But in the light of day, when I was face to face with him, I just couldn't bring myself to do it, to say anything. There was no amount of beer or pot I could have inside of me that would make a difference, that could give me the courage to say, *Blair, I want you, I want to kiss you and hold you, and run my tongue down your happy trail, and put your dick in my mouth.*

And so, he would drive me home and drop me off, give me a friendly wave at the foot of the driveway, and then drive off. I would stand there in the yellow light from the street

lamp, watching his tail lights disappear down the street before I would go into the house and go to bed and miss him.

You just need some experience.

But where would I get it from? And with whom?

"I won't be in class tomorrow, so I won't be picking you
up," Blair said one Wednesday night as he dropped me off.
"Just come by the house after class, and we can hang out
then."

"Why aren't you coming to class?" I asked. Blair was very
serious about attendance. I was always ready and willing to
skip class every day to spend it with him. But Blair always
insisted: "You can pull a C just by showing up every day."

"Because I have a doctor's appointment—nothing serious," he added hastily when he saw the look on my face.
"Just a check-up, that's all, I've been putting it off for a long
time and Mom goes nuts on me about shit like that, so I'm
going in tomorrow." He scowled. "I keep telling her I'll do
it when I go back to LA in a couple of weeks, but—"

"You're going back to LA?" My heart sank to my feet. It
was the first I'd heard of these plans.

"Well, yeah. Summer session's over, so I'm going to go
stay with my dad for a few weeks." He gave me a funny
look. "It's not the end of the world, you know. You can still
come by the house every day—everyone likes you, you're a
shoo-in to get a bid during rush—and it's only for a few
weeks until school starts again."

"So you'll be gone during my birthday?" I felt incredibly
betrayed, and struggled to keep a handle on my emotions.

"It's not that big . . ." he sighed. "Look, we'll talk about
this sometime when you're not so stoned, okay?"

I got out of the car and slammed the door. He sat there a
moment, looking at me, before he finally shrugged and

drove off. Almost immediately, I was sorry. I got out my cell phone and almost called—but then decided it wasn't a good idea. And besides, was it so wrong to be disappointed that my so-called best friend wouldn't be in town for my birthday? Was he really so selfish that he couldn't understand why that would bother me?

He doesn't really like you, that voice kept telling me as I undressed, *otherwise he wouldn't be gone for your birthday. And he never once mentioned that he was going home for a few weeks after summer session ended. Never once, and he had plenty of opportunities. You're not really his friend. You're just someone to hang out with until everyone comes back this fall.*

I didn't sleep well that night. I kept alternating between hurt and anger, would start to drift off to sleep after a while—and then my mind would start up again.

Just come by the house and hang out, everyone likes you.

Doesn't he understand the only reason I even go over there is for him?

I finally decided, *Fuck him, I'll come home after class.*

And then I was finally able to go to sleep.

But once class was over and I was in my car, I found myself driving over to the house. *I'll just see if he's there and if he's not, I won't stay.*

The Lexus wasn't in the parking lot, but I drove in anyway.

I parked the car and got out. I stood there for a minute, debating, and then decided to just go ahead and go inside and wait.

I waved up at Jerry in the window and he waved back down to me with a smile. *I can always get high with Jerry*, I thought as I went into the downstairs hall.

"Hey man, Blair's not here," Rory Armagh called as I walked past his room.

I stopped and walked back to his door. "Blair's not the only reason I come by the house, ya know," I said with a big smile. "I'm going to pledge."

"That's cool, man. Beta Kappa's a great house—best one on campus, don't let anyone tell you different." Rory was lying on his bed with his big hands behind his head. He was only wearing a pair of white BVD's, which did nothing to disguise the huge bulge. I tried to keep my eyes on his face. "You wanna get high, bro?" he asked. "I got some killer stuff from my guy last night."

I shrugged. "Sure." *Why the hell not? Be nice to have a buzz when Blair gets here.*

"Shut the door then."

I stepped inside and shut the door behind me, reaching for a towel to place under it. It was silly, but smoking pot inside the house was a $250 fine. Everyone assured me it was never enforced, but it was on the books because the university required it. "We have to have a strict no-drug policy," Jerry had said, rolling his eyes when I asked him about it. "Just like we're not allowed to let underage people drink."

The drug rules were disregarded completely by every house on fraternity row. Everyone referred to Sigma Chi, just across the mall for example, as Sigma High. Legend held that Sigma Alpha Epsilon parties were always full of high school-age girls, getting drunk and getting laid.

No, all you had to do, everyone assured me, was try to make sure the smell wasn't too obvious in the hallway and no one cared. Everyone smoked, so unless it was totally obvious, or a parent was in the house, no one turned anyone else in. All you needed to do was put a towel across the foot of the door to block the smoke, and if you really wanted to cover it up, light incense.

After I had finished putting the towel in its place, I straightened back up. Rory hadn't bothered to put on shorts or anything, and was holding what had to be the biggest bong I had ever seen. It stood on the floor at least three feet high between his legs, and had at least three chambers and scores of little plastic tubes running between them. He grinned at me. "You've never smoked out of the monster, have you?"

"No," I replied, my eyes wide.

"You are about to officially become initiated into the stoner fraternity. This ride is not for small-fry." He was loading pot into five bowls that sat in the front of the huge contraption. All five of the bowls were carved into a single piece of round metal. He winked at me. "Watch carefully, and learn . . . and don't feel bad if you can't handle it at first. Even I had trouble the first time."

I sat down beside him on the ratty love seat as he flicked a lighter to flame and bent his head down over the mouth. He started inhaling as he held the lighter to one bowl, and the lowest chamber filled with smoke. He then deftly lifted the round piece of metal, and turned it so another bowl went into the tubing, and burned it, still inhaling. Smoke snaked from the first chamber through two pipes into another chamber. He then switched in another bowl, still inhaling, as the smoke moved from the second chamber into a third—and finally, as he switched the fourth bowl in, into the final chamber. He turned his head, exhaled, and then put his mouth back on top of the bong. He inhaled for longer than I thought humanly possible and raised his head, placing one hand over the opening. He smiled at me, opened his mouth, and blew out a gigantic cumulus cloud. "Gooooood stuff." He passed the contraption over to me, his hand still over the top. "When I take my hand off, just put your mouth down and inhale as deep and as long as you can. You got it?"

I nodded and did as ordered. As I inhaled, I could feel the smoke moving down my throat into my lungs. It was pungent, more pungent than what Blair usually had—or the other brothers, for that matter—and it tasted green some-how. I sat back and stared at the ceiling for a few seconds before my lungs rebelled and the smoke poured out of me in a huge cloud. I kept coughing until Rory swatted me on the back and handed me a bottle of water.

"Dude, that was a swimmer's hit." He grinned at me, nod-ding. "Bro, I really mean it—that was fucking impressive. And Blair said you only started smoking this summer? Cool. You had to have been a swimmer at some point."

"No, I don't know how to swim, but thanks." I grinned back at him, my eyes watering. I took another swig of water. "Damn, that's some good stuff." My head was already start-ing to float away.

"Yeah." He nodded. "Water polo players, man, we get the good stuff all the time. One of the guys on the team is from Humboldt, another from Chico, man. That's where the best stuff comes from, unless you can get some Thai somewhere." He kept nodding. "So, you definitely gonna pledge, man?"

"Yeah. I kind of like it here."

"You're going to fit in just fine." Rory grinned over at me. He picked up a remote and flicked it at the stereo, and Pink Floyd's *The Wall* started playing. "Nothing better for a buzz than some Floyd."

"Cool." Everyone liked Pink Floyd at Beta Kappa—sometimes it seemed like something by them was playing somewhere in the house at every moment. I'd never really listened to it before, but I was becoming fond of Pink Floyd. The song playing was "Comfortably Numb," which was becoming my favorite. It described in music exactly the way I felt when I was stoned. "Can I ask you something? Do you mind? It's kind of personal."

"You're gonna be a brother, man, so sure. Ask me anything."

"Did you really—" I hesitated. "Did you really do porn?"

Rory threw his head back and laughed. "Man, oh man, did Blair tell you about that? I am going to kick his ass." He winked at me. "Just one weekend. I spent one weekend in Sacramento making some cash and it's going to haunt me for the rest of my life." He shook his head. "You know, this guy comes up to me after a water polo match, and gives me his card. Asks me if I want to make some easy cash. I just put it away, you know, didn't think nothing of it. Then last summer I was broke and needed to make some money—and I found the card. So I went up there for a weekend, fucked some chicks on camera, and made some money. Is that some crazy shit or what?"

"I think it's kind of cool." I shrugged.

"You wanna see?" His eyes lit up. "Nobody around here's seen it besides me."

"Seriously?"

"Sure!" He winked at me. "Love to hear what you think of my performance."

"Um, I've never really seen a porn movie before," I replied, "So I really don't have a frame of reference."

"You've got to be shitting me! Where are you from,

Kansas or something? Dude, porn is awesome! What do you beat off to?"

I didn't answer that, assuming he didn't expect an answer. I mean, I seriously doubted he cared what I beat off to—and it wasn't like I was going to tell him anyway. He grabbed another remote and turned the TV on, muted the sound so as not to compete with the Pink Floyd CD, and then clicked another button. Suddenly, the heavily made-up weeping woman from *As the World Turns* was replaced by a large-breasted woman in a string bikini and stiletto heels sitting by a swimming pool reading *People* magazine. A gate in the wooden fence opened, and there was Rory, looking about twenty years younger than the woman, wearing only a pair of baggy shorts. He walked over to where she was sitting, they apparently spoke a few words to each other, and then she unzipped his shorts and started sucking his cock.

My eyes about popped out of my head.

If I thought it was huge when limp, well, it was gigantic when hard.

Almost inhuman.

"They keep calling me, wanting me to do more," Rory said as he sat back down on the bed. "I guess they like my big ol' dick. But you know, I don't need the money, and it would be just my luck to make the Olympic team and then have this come out, you know? Porn always seems to come back to bite you in the ass."

I glanced over at Rory on the bed. His eyes were transfixed on the screen, and he was stroking himself through his underwear. He looked over at me, and smiled. "It kind of turns me on watching myself, you know? Do you think that's weird?"

I swallowed, and looked back at the television screen.

"Um, no, I don't. I mean, I guess not. I don't know if I'd get turned on watching myself."

"Sure you would! You've got a nice body, man."

"You think so?"

"Sure, man." He looked over at me. "Really nice, in shape. Good looking too. The little sisters are going to line up to suck your dick, man. That's one of the benefits of the house you know. The house whores."

"Um, okay."

He patted the bed beside him. "Why don't you come sit over here?"

I took a deep breath and walked over to the bed. *This isn't happening*, I kept saying to myself over and over, *this isn't happening*. I looked at his crotch. The head of his cock was sticking out through the waistband of his BVD's. It was big, so big and thick and red. A single clear drop oozed out of the slit.

"You want to help a brother out and suck me off?" he whispered.

You wanted experience—here's your chance.

"Um . . . I don't know . . ."

"I won't tell anyone. It's just between us." He pulled the waistband down, and I couldn't believe my eyes. His balls were thick and heavy, and the cock—it had to be eleven, twelve inches long and a minimum of six around.

"I—I—"

"I won't come in your mouth," he whispered. "Come on, Jeff, no one will know."

I sat down on the side of the bed. My entire body was trembling. I leaned over, took a deep breath, and put my hand on it. It was so warm, and Rory moaned a little bit.

"Just suck it, man, put it in your mouth. I won't tell any-one."

I closed my eyes and put the head in my mouth.

It tasted slightly salty, sweaty with a slight tinge of chlo-rine.

Of course it's chlorine, dumb ass, he's a swimmer!

I started licking the head.

"Oh, man, that's nice, Jeff, yeah, keep doing that."

I started licking it, not really knowing what I was doing. Out of the corner of my eye I glanced at the porn video playing. She was sucking his cock, and if that nasty looking old whore could do it, so could I.

I started moving my mouth up and down on it, but couldn't get that far.

I looked over at the screen. *How the hell was she—*

And then I remembered something from a party in Kansas. Two guys were talking about shooting a beer, "You have to open your throat, man, then everything just goes pouring straight down . . ."

Open your throat.

I focused on an upward movement, and then as I came back down again, I opened my throat and it went down.

"Ooooooh fuck man!" Rory's hips started moving, and he gripped my hair with both hands.

I found myself getting into it. I loved the taste of his cock in my mouth, I loved the power I had over him. I was con-trolling this great big hunk of man. I was sucking him off like a pro, and it was the first fucking time I'd ever given a blow job. I began using my tongue, and put my hand around the base to keep it in place. I started moving faster and faster, and then he was pulling my head away, yanking me by the hair, and I was angry.

I didn't want to stop, goddamnit!

And his entire body arched and shook as he shot a huge load onto his stomach and chest, his body heaving with each shot.

And when he was finished, he closed his eyes and laid there for a moment.

I wiped at my mouth. I could still taste him. . . . I wanted to keep on. . . .

"Thanks bud." He opened his eyes and smiled at me. He picked up the remote and switched the television off. "You mind? I'm going to take a nap."

"Sure. Yeah." I got up, my cheeks flaming with embarrassment. *What have I done?*

I shut the door behind me and walked back into the parking lot.

What have I done?

Somehow, I managed to get to my car and drive home.

And no matter how much I brushed my teeth, I could still taste his cock.

Chapter 4

I skipped class the next day.

I didn't want to face Blair, or any of the other students. I felt like there was a gigantic sign on my forehead flashing in red neon to everyone *COCKSUCKER! COCKSUCKER! COCKSUCKER!* I told my mother I didn't feel good and just went to my room and shut the door. She checked in on me a few times—once to tell me Blair was on the phone—and I just said I don't want to talk to anyone, and after that she left me alone. I'd turned my cell phone off, and just lay in bed staring at the ceiling.

Now you've done it. You're a homo for sure.

There's no turning back now.

I wasn't sure how I felt about it, now that I'd actually done it. There was always that part in the back of my mind which always insisted it was just a phase; as long as I never acted on it I'd be okay. All I needed to do was fuck a girl and I'd snap out of it. But that didn't keep me from longing for boys—Kevin, then Blair—and now I'd actually done it—*something*—with another guy, it was with a guy I barely knew, someone I certainly wasn't in love with, so what did that make me?

Not only a queer, but a *slut.*

I couldn't face anyone. All I wanted to do was stay in my room for the rest of my life and hide from the rest of the world. I woke up in the middle of the night and left a message on Blair's cell phone, telling him I wasn't coming to class *(ever again)* so he wouldn't show up in the morning. When my mom came to wake me up, I told her I still didn't feel so hot and I wasn't going. She shut the door and went away.

At noon, my door opened again.

"I'm not hungry," I said without looking.

"What the hell is wrong with you?" Blair walked in and sat down on the edge of the bed.

"Nothing. Go away."

"Jesus fucking Christ on the cross, Jeff, I'm the drama major, remember? You're the writer." He lit a cigarette. My mother didn't allow anyone else to smoke in the house. "Now, tell me what the hell is going on. You're supposed to meet me at the house yesterday; I get there and there was no sign of you. You don't answer your phone. Your mother tells me you're not well. This morning I get this pathetic voicemail that you're not coming to class. Tell me what's wrong."

"I don't want to talk about it."

"So you sucked Rory Armagh's cock? It's not the end of the world."

I sat up in bed. "Did he tell you that?"

Blair laughed. "He didn't have to." He put an arm around me. "And he isn't going to tell anyone else, either, if that's what you're so afraid of. The last thing in the world Rory Armagh is going to do is let *anyone* know another guy sucked him off. You can put that in the bank and collect interest on it, okay?"

"How—how did you know?"

"You think *I* haven't sucked Rory off?" He started laughing. "Don't you remember what I told you that first day at the house? Straight boys don't care who gets them off when they're fucked up, remember? And alcohol, or pot, or coke, or whatever, is a perfect excuse for them." He rolled his eyes. "'Oh, man I was so fucked up last night, I think I let some guy suck my dick' or 'Oh man was I drunk last night, I think I fucked some guy up the ass'. Whatever. The truth is Rory would let a *dog* suck his dick if he was horny. And by dog, I don't mean an ugly girl. I mean a dog. A cocker spaniel. A Great Dane. Get the picture?"

"I—I guess."

"Look." He dropped the cigarette into an empty Coke can on my nightstand, and grabbed me by the shoulders. "You're my friend, okay? I don't know if you're gay, straight, whatever you are—that doesn't matter. What matters to me is you're cool, and a nice guy, and a lot of fun to hang out with, okay? I want you to join Beta Kappa because I think you'll have a good time there. The guys are pretty cool for the most part, and we have the best parties. Just because you sucked Rory Armagh's dick when you were wasted one night doesn't mean anything, you got that? All it means was you were curious about it . . . and sexual curiosity is not a bad thing or a big deal."

"I don't like girls, Blair," I said in a small voice. I couldn't look at him as I said it; I'd never said it out loud before.

He lit another cigarette. "Yeah? So what?"

"I think I might be gay." I said the words, and let out a big sigh of relief. I'd been fighting it for so long, denying it for as long as I could remember. So what if it meant I couldn't join Beta Kappa? So what if it meant losing Blair as a friend?

But he kissed you, he sat on top of you and rubbed on you . . .

"Like I said, Jeff, so fucking what?" He laughed again. "I grew up around the film industry, for God's sake. You have any idea how many gays and lesbians I know? Hell, my mom is bisexual—she has a girlfriend right now over in London! You need to get past this idea that it's a bad thing to be gay, honey. It's not." He took my hand. "Look at me." I met his eyes. "I am sure growing up in Kansas—and your parents are nice enough people, but they don't seem to be the most open-minded people in the world, no offense— was pretty hard on you. I can't even imagine it. But being gay is not a sin or wrong or whatever you think it is, my friend. It's just who you are. Do you really, deep down, think you're a bad person?"

"No," I said slowly. "No, I don't."

"Because you aren't, you big dope. You're still Jeff. That hasn't changed at all. You understand? You are still Jeff to me, and you're still Jeff to everyone—and anyone who wants to not like you or think there's something wrong with you—well, that's *their* problem, not yours. Am I making sense here?" He puffed on the cigarette. "Am I?"

"Some." I did feel relieved that Blair didn't turn on me— but then again, that night in his room, he had been the one to initiate things between us, even though he'd also been the one to stop. "Blair, are *you* gay?"

He shook his head. "You are something else, you know that, Kansas boy?" He leaned over and kissed my cheek.

"Yes, yes, I am gay. I don't like girls either." He shuddered. "Blech. Those big old boobs? Them big old hips? And don't even get me started on vaginas." He grinned at me. "Nope, I'm a big old fairy."

"Then why"—I hesitated, then plunged forward—"why didn't you want to be with me that time? I mean . . ." my voice trailed off.

"Oh, you big dope." He started laughing again. "Don't tell me—oh, this is priceless." He leaned over and brushed my cheek with his lips. "Jeff, I am very attracted to you. Are you kidding me? Have you looked in a fucking mirror lately? Let's see, hmmm. Okay. You're about what, six two? Blond, blue-eyed, and tan. You have an amazing body, and you have this seductively innocent look about you . . . porn directors would drool over you. You could be an escort and pay your way through school—if you only knew what you were doing."

"Then why didn't you want me?" I couldn't help myself, I knew I was pouting like a little kid.

"Oh, God in heaven." He threw his arms up in the air. "Jeff." He took my face in both hands. "You're the kind of guy I could fall in love with," he whispered. "Don't you get it? The last thing in the world I wanted to be was just one of those . . . oh, shit." He laughed and bit his lips. "I wanted it to be *special* for us, if it was meant to be, does that make sense? If you were one of those horny fucked up straight boys who just wanted to get off with whoever happened to be handy—I didn't want that, and you said yourself you'd never been with a guy before."

"That wasn't true." I admitted, my heart singing, *He wants me! He wants me!*

An eyebrow went up. "What do you mean it wasn't true? You lied to me?"

I nodded. "I—I didn't want to admit it, even to you. But I've been with a guy before."

There was a park in Emporia, near the campus of the university there. One night, Kevin and I and the girls we were going steady with at the time were driving around, aimlessly looking for something to do, some place to park and maybe make out or something. The movie was over, we'd eaten, and there was nothing else for us to do. The girls didn't have to be home until midnight, and we had some time to kill. I started to pull the Flying Couch over at the park when the girl I was dating—Lisa Driscoll—shrieked, "We can't park here!"

"Why not?" I looked over at her.

"This is a park where the queers go." She curled her lip. "You know . . . to do whatever it is they do."

"How do you know that?"

"My sister goes to E-State, and she told me to never come here at night. Everyone knows about it. Get us out of here!"

So, I'd driven off. But a week later, when I didn't have a date, I came back by myself. I parked my car a few blocks away from the park—in case someone I knew drove by—and walked over. My hands were sweating, my stomach churning, and I was scared to death. What if the cops are there? What if someone I know sees me? What if . . . what if . . . what if . . . the thoughts kept swirling around in my head as I approached the park. It was dark and cloudy; there was very little light once you got away from the street lamps. I crossed the street and walked into the park. I couldn't see anyone around, and wondered if Lisa had been wrong, if I was wasting my time. What if I was too early? What if I was too late? Were there really other queers in Emporia? I walked through the park in my tight jeans and my T-shirt, my eyes darting around to try to see signs of life, of anyone, of anything. I kept walking, around trees and over grass, and after about a half an hour I was pretty certain I was wasting my time.

"Okay, just go home." I said to myself as I walked into a small clearing where the restrooms were located. I glanced at my watch. 11:15. I had forty-five minutes to get back home before curfew. I sighed. I'd wasted my night. All those nerves, everything—all for nothing.

"Hey."

I jumped, and looked as a man emerged from the bushes to my right. He was short, maybe about five six, with a mustache and longish blond hair. He was wearing a tank top and a ratty looking pair of jeans, and his body was lean and tight. "Hey." I said, wondering if he was a serial killer or something worse.

"How ya doin?" He lit a cigarette, and in the flare of his lighter I saw that he was unshaven, and there was a Marine tattoo on his right arm.

"Okay."

He walked over closer to me, and smiled at me. He was maybe thirty years old. "What ya lookin for, kid?"

I swallowed, and fought the urge to turn and run. "I'm looking for a man," I said, hoping against hope he wasn't going to beat me up—but then again, I was taller and heavier.

"You've found one." He stepped up close to me, and put his hand on my crotch. He grinned up at me. "Nice." He made a head gesture. "I'm parked over there."

"Okay."

I followed him out to a van. He unlocked the back and climbed in. Looking around to make sure there was no one around, I climbed in and shut the doors behind me. The back of the van was carpeted, and there was a toolbox off to one side. He started brushing toys to the side, and crazy thoughts went through my head. *He's married, he has kids, this isn't right, this is wrong, I need to get out of here while I still can . . .*

He pulled his tank top over his head and smiled at me. "Come here, boy."

I reached out and touched his chest. It was mostly smooth, except for some errant hairs around each nipple. "Take your shirt off," he instructed, so I pulled my shirt up off over my head. "Aren't you a pretty boy?" He leaned over and put his lips on my right nipple, and started sucking it.

My breath started coming in gasps. I'd never felt anything like this before—it felt incredible. My cock got harder in my pants, and my head went back as I moaned. None of the girls I'd ever dated had ever let me do more than kiss them or get my hand up inside their shirt. They'd certainly never touched my dick, they'd never sucked my nipples. Then he moved his mouth over to my other nipple and I thought I was going to come right then and there. He looked up at me with his eyes and winked. One of his hands went down to my crotch and undid my belt, then the fly of my jeans. I lifted my ass up so he could yank my underwear and pants down. He took his mouth off my nipple and smiled at me. "Damn, that's a big cock, boy, do you know how to use it?"

"Uh-huh," was all I managed to get out.

He smiled again and stood up, pulling his own pants down. He didn't have on any underwear, and his own dick was standing up straight away from the thick blond hair. He opened the toolbox and grabbed a condom, which he opened and rolled over my dick. My dick jerked when he touched it, but he grabbed it at the base and squeezed. "Not ready for that yet, boy." He grinned at me, then squirted something on it. He reached down and pinched my right nipple. "Okay, boy time to show me what you can do with that big ol' club you got." He straddled me and grabbed my dick, and then slowly started sitting on it.

I could barely breathe. It felt amazing. Much better than when I beat myself off, much better than when I humped a pillow—the moist wet tightness of his asshole seemed to simply grab on to my cock and hold on to it. He gasped and stopped. "Damn, boy you've got a big one, don't you? That's gonna take me some time to get used to."

"Oh—oh—okay."

Finally, with the occasional grunt and moan, he managed to get all of me inside of him, and started rocking on it a little bit. "Boy, that feel so fucking good inside of me, you like it up there in my ass?"

"Oh God, yes."

He slid up slowly, and then settled back down. "I wanna keep that big ol' thing inside me as long as I can, boy," he whispered down at me.

"Uh-huh." I didn't care as long as it kept feeling this good.

He started moving faster, and stroking himself. It was like nothing I'd ever felt before—the friction on my dick, the feel of his hard little ass settling on my balls on the way down, the sliding of my dick out of him, and his hard little body looked so damned good up there, riding me. And then I felt it starting—"I'm gonna come." I gasped out.

"Good. Shoot it up inside me!"

My entire body went rigid and started trembling as an almost painful pressure started building inside of me and then I screamed as it started pumping out of me . . . and he moaned as his own started squirting out of him. We both kept gasping, moaning and convulsing—and then I was finished . . . and my body trembled as I tried to catch my breath.

"Nice," he said, reaching down with a towel and wiping himself off of me. He got off me and peeled the condom off, which he wrapped in a paper towel and put in a garbage bag. He handed me my T-shirt as he pulled up his own pants. "Thanks, boy." He opened the back doors to the van as I fastened my pants. I climbed out the back, holding my shirt.

"Thanks, kid." He winked and shut the car doors. As I stood there, the van started and then pulled away.

I put my shirt back on and headed back to my car.

Blair started laughing. "You had anonymous sex with some married closet case in a park?"

"Don't laugh at me!" I pushed him away from me. "It's not funny!"

"And here I thought you were this innocent little boy from the prairies." He stood up. He looked at me, his eyes sparkling. "I've got a great idea. What are you doing this weekend?"

"Nothing."

"Let's go to LA!"

I goggled at him. "Los Angeles?"

"Yeah." He started bouncing on the bed. "We can stay at my dad's—and we can hang out, and I can show you around. It'll be a blast!" he jumped off the bed. "Pack some clothes, dude. I'll go fix it up with your mom!" He paused at my bedroom door. "Get ready to live, prairie boy!"

Chapter 5

"Hell of a party, huh?" Blair grinned over at me.

"Uh-huh." I collapsed on the gigantic bed, wasted out of my mind. I'd been smoking pot and drinking beer all day, and the bed felt incredible. My mind was still kind of spinning from everything that had happened since we'd gotten to Los Angeles the day before.

I still couldn't believe I was in Los Angeles—Beverly Hills, to be exact. It had taken us four hours to get down the highway from Polk to the big city—and Blair had laughed at me constantly that first day. "Close your mouth, you're gonna draw flies," he kept saying over and over as he drove me through Hollywood, showing me the landmarks I'd dreamed of when I was growing up in Kansas. After showing me around there, he had veered up Santa Monica Boulevard and taken me into West Hollywood—"WeHo," he'd called it, "the gayest place in Southern California." And he wasn't kidding. It seemed like everywhere I looked I saw beautiful gay men, holding hands, sitting outside coffee shops, waiting in line to get into restaurants, or just walking along the sidewalk. He took me to a gay bookstore

called A Different Light, and showed me books and maga-
zines I'd never dreamed existed. He introduced me to the
manager, a hot man wearing tight jeans and a tank top, with
a ripped body covered with tattoos. He bought me dinner at
a restaurant a few blocks away, and the waiter was one of
the most beautiful men I'd ever seen. After he'd taken our
order and left us, I said as much to Blair.

"Probably an actor," Blair shrugged. "Beautiful men are a
dime a dozen down here."

I want to live here, kept running through my mind over
and over again. *Once I get my degree, I am moving down here.*

And after dinner, he drove me up to a huge beautiful
building in Beverly Hills, where we were let in by a security
guard. The house was like a Moorish castle, with fountains
spread out all over the lawn, and massive palm trees casting
shade here and there. "Welcome to my dad's," Blair said as
he parked the car. "We have the whole place to ourselves—
Dad's in Prague making his latest epic movie."

He showed me through the house—which looked like a
museum. I couldn't keep my mouth shut—drawing flies—
on the tour. There were at least ten bedrooms, and from
Blair's bedroom a set of French doors led to a balcony that
overlooked an Olympic sized pool, surrounded by columns
and marble statuary. As I stood out there, on that starry
night looking out over the lights of the city of Los Angeles
spread out below me, I felt tears coming to my eyes.

Blair put an arm around me. "Being Steve Blanchard's
son has its perks, huh?"

"How—how could you live in the Beta Kappa house
after living here?" I finally managed to stammer out. "My
parents' whole house could fit in your bedroom."

Blair sparked a joint and passed it to me. "A bit of an exaggeration, which I've noticed you're prone to. It's rather endearing, though, my friend." He shrugged. "I've been in boarding schools, too, you know, so having a cubicle of a room isn't a big deal to me. And besides, Mom's house in London is pretty small. All this"—he made a sweeping motion with his arms, taking in the house and the grounds— "overwhelms me a bit from time to time. A rather vulgar and ostentatious display of wealth, as my mother would say."

"Yeah, well, I could learn to like it." I took a deep hit and passed the joint.

"Eh." He made a face. "It's not as much fun as it looks. When Dad's here"—he pointed to the wall that ran around the grounds—"there's always the paparazzi outside the gates, or hanging in the trees trying to get pictures. That sucks." He laughed. "I used to moon them every once in a while, just to see if they'd print it since I was underage. They didn't—because Dad would have charged them with kiddie porn." He sighed. "Ah, the lifestyles of the rich and famous aren't what they're cracked up to be, are they?"

We stayed up late, smoking another joint and drinking a bottle of wine from his father's wine cellar—he told me the name and year, but it meant nothing to me—before falling into bed together. When he told me we'd both sleep in his room, I wondered if this was the night it would happen— but it didn't. Blair stripped down to his black Versace underwear, climbed into bed and rolled over onto his side. I lay there for a while, listening to him breathe, watching his back and wanting so desperately to reach out and touch him, to put my arms around him, cuddle up with him. Instead, I turned onto my side with my back to him and fell into a restless sleep.

* * *

"I think we're going to have a party tonight," Blair said, waking me up the next morning with a cup of coffee and a toasted bagel smeared with cream cheese. He'd already showered and put on a pair of shorts.

I sat up and took a bite of the bagel. "A party?"

"Yeah." He smiled at me. "I can get my dad's caterer to deliver some food and liquor, and I can call up some people I know—we can have an impromptu pool party. Swim suits required." He leered at me. "I have a bikini you can borrow. Besides, you need to meet some gay people, I think."

"A bikini?" I stared at him. "Oh, no, Blair, I don't think—"

"Gay or bi or confused or whatever it is you are, you need to stop being ashamed of your body," he said, getting up and opening the French doors. Bright sunshine spilled in, a few wispy clouds danced slowly across an azure blue sky. "It's a perfect day for a pool party—and if you don't wear a bikini, you'll be the only one. Finish your food and get out of bed."

I did as I was told, gulping down the bagel in a few bites and washing it down with the coffee, which was good and strong. A little nervously, I got out of the bed. He looked at me critically. "Nice." He smiled. "The tan line needs work—but I know what we can do about that."

"What's wrong with it?" I asked, looking down at my legs.

"Your tan line stops about an inch or so above your knees." He shook his head. "That's a very Kansas-boy tan line. But then again," he folded his arms, raised an eyebrow and cocked his head to one side, "that's exactly who you should be at the party."

"What are you talking about?" I asked, shifting from one foot to the other.

"Oh, yes." He walked over to a dresser, pulled open a drawer and started rummaging through it. He pulled out a bright red bathing suit and placed it on top of the dresser. He started humming as he went through the drawer, and eventually two other suits—one yellow, one pale blue— joined the red one. He turned and tossed them to me. "Try these on."

I caught them and put them down on the bed. There didn't seem to be much material for any of them. "Um, I don't know—"

"Honey, let me explain something to you once and for all about being gay." He rolled his eyes. "Just call me Obi-wan." He laughed. "Oh, I crack myself *up*. The most important thing about being a gay man—and a good one—that most gay men never seem to understand is"—he walked over to me, put a hand on my shoulder, and leaned in, adding in a whisper—"it's all in the marketing."

"Huh?" He wasn't making any sense to me.

He reached over and picked up the red bikini. "Here, try this one on." He gave me a wicked grin. "Do you want me to look away?"

I blushed. "No," I said, trying to sound defiant. "You can look all you want."

"In that case"—he took a few steps away from me and folded his arms—"go for it, prairie boy."

I slid my underwear down, stepping out of it and standing in front of him stark naked. I reached for the pale blue pair, making sure he could see my naked ass as I bent over the bed. I stepped into them and pulled them up. They were not my size; I'm bigger than Blair—but even on Blair, they wouldn't have covered a whole hell of a lot. I somehow

managed to tuck my cock and my balls inside the little tri-
angle of fabric, and turned back to him. "Well?"

"We're going to need to trim your pubic hair for sure," he
said, stepping close. "Turn around, let me see your ass." I
obliged, catching a glimpse of myself in the full mirror on
the wall beside the bed. I blushed again—surely he couldn't
want me to go out in front of people wearing something this
revealing—but I stood there for a moment as he adjusted
the suit over my ass, I started to see myself in a completely
different way. The suit *was* sexy; and while I'd never really
given a lot of thought to my cock size, the pale blue made it
look rather large. Nothing as large as Rory Armagh's—he
was practically deformed—but I kind of had to smile. I
raised my arms and flexed my biceps.

Yeah, I looked hot.

But I could also see what he meant about my tan line and
my pubic hair. Hair was coming out of the suit on every
side, and it looked, well, *sloppy*. And the tan line looked
ridiculous in this suit. I'd always worn long shorts whenever
I was swimming or doing anything in the sun, so the skin
below my knees was a dark, rich brown. Above my knees
was as white as my ass. That skin had never seen the sun,
and the skimpy bikini made it very apparent.

"Okay, put on the yellow," he instructed. He walked over
to his desk and sat down. He started rolling a joint.

I was a little disappointed that he wasn't going to watch
me change—God, how I wanted him to look at me—but I
pulled the pale blue suit off. I pulled on the yellow, making
the same adjustments in the front as I had before, and then
looked over my shoulder at my ass in the mirror. I started
adjusting the backside. "Jesus, I have a big ass," I said aloud.

"You have a hot ass." Blair finished rolling the joint and looked over at me. "I like the yellow better than the blue."

"The blue made my dick look huge."

"So does the yellow." He lit the joint. "Face it, my love, you have a big dick and a hot ass. Put the red on." I did as he took a hit. Once I had finished adjusting myself, he gave me a big grin. "And we have a winner! Red, my dear, is definitely your color."

"You think?" I took the joint from him and took a big hit.

"Oh, yes." He nodded. "You're going to make a big splash tonight at my little party."

I spent the rest of the day grooming. Blair taught me how to put gel in my hair; how to shave my balls, and he also decided that I needed to shave my chest and underarms. "Are you sure I need to do this?" I looked at him dubiously. My balls already were bare, and I had trimmed down the rest of my pubic hair with electric clippers. "I mean, I kind of like that hair."

"It's all in the marketing, darlin'," he replied. "Yes, I'm sure. The smoother you are, the more they will like you. It will make you look even younger than you already do—and we're selling you as a farm boy from Kansas right off the bus."

"What do you mean by sell?" I started lathering the spot in the middle of my chest where all my hair was located.

"I don't mean I am going to pimp you out, if that's what you're afraid of." He burst out laughing. "Lord! No, honey, you're a product—remember? All of us are products, and we have to make ourselves as desirable as we can. We package ourselves into the most appealing product for as many different consumers as we can. And I don't mean that we have to sleep with all of them—no, just being desired is the end result we want, always. As long as you remember that—you'll go far. Now finish shaving off that hair, I need to call the caterers."

I spent the rest of the day by myself, with Blair poking his head in every once in a while to check on my progress. Around six, he sent me to his father's workout room to "pump up", which felt kind of silly to me. I'd been lifting weights ever since junior high for sports, and I'd never really thought about weight lifting as anything other than a way to improve my athletic performance—and once I was out of high school, I was done with it. But every wall in Steve Blanchard's workout room, which was better equipped than the one at Southern Heights, was mirrored. And as I did curls with a pair of twenty pound dumbbells, I watched as the veins in my arms popped out, and once I set the weights down, I realized my biceps did look better. I heard Blair saying, *"it's all in the marketing"* in my head, and I began to understand what he meant. He thought I looked good—but I could look better. And looking better was what it was all about. I decided then and there to start working out at CSUP's gym when we got back on Monday.

I showered after pumping up, and slipped back into the red bikini, staring at myself in the mirror. Now, I felt kind of self-conscious about the long stretch of white skin from the bottom of the swimsuit to just above the knee. But my chest gleamed in the bathroom lights, and I raised my arms to inspect my underarms, which were white and pristine. They stung a little bit as well, but Blair said that would pass. My muscles were all pumped up. No errant long curly hairs were sticking out of the bikini anywhere.

I looked sexy.

The bathroom door opened and Blair whistled. "Damn,

boy, you are one hot stud." A joint was dangling from his mouth. "Just wanted to let you know people are starting to arrive. Almost time for your grand entrance." He gave me that evil grin I loved so much. "And just for the record, you're mine, okay? No sneaking off to get fucked in the bushes—or a van—"

"Blair!"

"Just teasing you, dear." He brushed my cheek with his lips.

"Blair—"I hesitated.

"Yeah?"

"Thank you."

His face softened. "Oh, Jeff, you don't ever have to thank me. I hope you know that."

"No, I do." I sat down on the toilet seat. "Thank you. You've changed my life."

"I hope you mean that in a good way."

"Yeah, yeah I do." Maybe it was the pot I'd been smoking all day, or the occasional glasses of wine Blair brought me, but I felt like I was going to break down and cry. No one had ever been as sweet to me as Blair before. Kevin— well, Kevin had been my best friend back in Kansas, but I'd never dared to be honest with him about who I was. Blair knew who I was, knew the truth about me, and he cared about me anyway. He cared enough to bring me down to Los Angeles and introduce me to his friends. He cared enough about me to teach me about being gay. I felt tears bubbling up in my eyes.

"Oh, girl, don't cry." Blair slid an arm around me. "This is a party, and you can't be going down there all puffy-eyed." He kissed me on the cheek.

"I love you, Blair."

I felt him stiffen, and knew instinctively that I'd said the wrong thing. Without looking at him, I went on, "You're the best friend anyone could ever ask for. You're like my brother."

He relaxed, and I made a mental note—*never say I love you to him, no matter how much you mean it, he's not comfortable with that.* He stood up. "Now, dry your eyes and come down to the party. Do me proud."

"Okay." I stood up and smiled at him. "Let's party."

The evening passed in a blur. I'm sure I walked around with my mouth open in awe all night long, but I didn't care about the impression I was making on anyone. At its height, there were about fifty people there—all men, all gay, and all beautiful. I recognized one guy from an exercise infomercial I'd seen on a cable channel once for an ab machine, and he was stunningly beautiful. Another guy I recognized from a commercial for shaving cream, another from underwear ads, and so on. There was a guy who looked vaguely familiar to me—and then I realized when he was a kid he'd been on one of those live-action Saturday morning shows. Another guy with an amazing ass turned out to have been an Olympic figure skater. Everyone was beautiful, everyone was sexy, everyone was kind—and didn't seem to mind that I could never remember anyone's name. The figure skater just smiled as I apologized for forgetting his name and said, "It's okay, you're pretty dear. You can be forgiven almost everything—except giving crabs."

I got touched a lot, but never in an ugly or scary way. It was always just an appreciation of some sort—maybe that sounds naïve, but none of them touched with any ulterior motives, or so it seemed. Someone would come up to me and drape an arm over my shoulder while he made small talk, and maybe his hand would drop down and stroke my ass, but there was no follow-through, no requests for my phone number, no offer of theirs. It was, I don't know, nice. They asked me about myself, what I wanted to do with my life, and I couldn't *really* be from Kansas—was anyone really from there? But what might have seemed in a different tone of voice mean and condescending, was said in a teasing manner—and every Kansas remark was followed by "If they grow them like this in Kansas I'm taking the next bus to Topeka!"

Any self-consciousness I might have felt about my skimpy little bikini was gone within a few moments of joining the party. I had more on than most of the guests—many of whom were wearing glorified jockstraps that showed their asses.

And what beautiful asses they were!

Ordinarily, I would have worried about getting hard in the little bikini—but because there were so many beautiful men there, I was on overload. I couldn't stare at one for long before another one came into view who was just as gorgeous as the previous one. And everyone knew me as Blair's new friend Jeff, who'd just moved to California from Kansas.

"Have you ever done any modeling?" one man with long blond hair and a diamond stud in one ear asked me.

"No," was all I could think to respond.

"I'll give Blair one of my cards. Give me a call if you want to get started." He winked at me. "You could do quite well for yourself. I can just see you on a billboard."

I just laughed and moved on.

Others asked if I was an actor, if I wanted to do this or that, if I'd met so-and-so. And I was invited to other parties.

I just kept smiling and talking to people, meeting people, making small talk, chit-chatting, drinking champagne, and accepting hits off of joints.

And then it was just me and Blair again.

I was collapsed in a reclining deck chair, a half-full glass of champagne in my hand. I was more than a little drunk, and a lot stoned. "Did you have fun?" Blair asked as he collapsed into the chair next to mine. "You certainly made an impression on them all, as I knew you would."

"Oh, Blair." I rolled my head to the side so I could look at him. "Your friends are the nicest people."

"Well, let's not get crazy. They're fun—but I wouldn't go so far as to call them *nice*." Blair took a sip from his own glass, and then yawned. "You were quite a hit. *Everyone* wants you to call them, you know."

"Really?"

"Look at you, grinning from ear to ear." He smiled at me, then yawned. "No, you won't be calling any of them, you know."

"I won't?"

"Oh no, I warned them all off—you belong to me, remember? I told you."

"I wasn't sure if you meant it or not."

"Of course I meant it, silly little Jeff."

I didn't know what to say. I felt like crying a little bit.

"Come on, let's go up to bed." He reached out and took my hand, and I pulled him down on top of me, spilling his glass and mine. "Hey!"

I put my arms around him, and pulled his face down to mine and kissed him.

He resisted at first, but I could feel his dick starting to get hard against my stomach. He relaxed into the kiss, and it was like we went to a different place, as though we floated off the deck chairs and started drifting upward to the sky. I slid a hand down his back and cupped his hard ass with my hand. It tightened in my hand, and I slid my hand inside the bikini so I could feel his bare ass. His skin was velvety and smooth. He moved his head to the side, taking his lips down to my throat, and he started kissing me at the base. I moaned. It felt incredible, and then he was tracing designs on my throat with his tongue. He tilted his head back. "Come on, stud." He pushed himself up off of me and took me by the hand. "I don't want to do this outside, in case the paparazzi are around. I'm of age now. Come on, can you control yourself and that dick for a few minutes? Let's go up to my room."

My heart sang as he led me up to the bedroom. It was all I could do not to run up the stairs. *Blair and I are going to bed together, we're going to be lovers, my dreams are coming true!* Once we were inside, he pulled me into a deep kiss, his tongue exploring my mouth as his hands grabbed my ass and squeezed. He moved his head down my throat, nibbling on first one nipple, before moving on to the other as my knees buckled. It felt incredible, the pleasure was so intense I didn't know how long I could stand it. He bit down a little harder on the right one, and the shock of the pain along with the pleasure that followed was so much I almost fell down. I gasped out, "Oh God!"

My cock sprang through the waistband of my bikini, and when he got to his knees and took it in his mouth I thought the top of my head would blow off. He teased the head of my dick with his tongue, before running his tongue along the base, and taking my shaved balls into his mouth. I put both hands on his shoulders as I moaned, and looked down through half-open eyes. I looked into his eyes and he closed one eye in a wink as he slid his mouth back up my cock to the tip.

"That's . . . so . . . good," I gasped out. "My God, Blair, please, don't stop."

He winked again.

And then he took my entire cock in his mouth, all the way down to the base, and I moaned again. My heart was racing, I could hear it pounding in my ears as he slid his mouth back and forth slowly over my cock.

Nothing in my wildest dreams had ever prepared me for this sensation.

My whole body began to tremble.

And he stopped.

He closed his hand over the base of my cock and stood up. "I want you to come inside me, Jeff."

"Anything . . . anything you want, Blair," I breathed out between gasps.

"Anything?" he asked, one eyebrow arching upwards. "You better be careful who you say that to, my little prairie boy."

He let go of me and walked over to the bed, stripping out of his bikini on the way. He had no tan lines, his round hard little ass tanned as dark as the rest of him, and when he turned around I saw he'd shaved off his pubic hair. His entire body was smooth as silk, tanned a deep brown, and just beautiful to behold. The definition in his abs, the veins in his arms and shoulders, his muscular legs. I stared at him, wanting to always remember the way he looked as he stood there naked in front of me, and then he beckoned to me.

His own cock was erect, standing straight up along his torso. It was bigger than I would have thought, with a big head and getting thicker as it got closer to the base. He walked over to the nightstand and got out a brown bottle and a clear plastic bottle of Wet. He put them on top, and laid down on the bed, his legs spread. "Come here," he said.

I walked over as he tore open a condom wrapper. He squirted some of the lube inside, and rolled it down over the top of my cock. He squirted more lube on my now-encased dick, and squirted some in his hand. He reached down and lubed up his ass. He opened the brown bottle and inhaled, before offering it to me.

"What is it?" I asked.

"Poppers. Don't worry—it won't hurt you."

I inhaled up one nostril, then up the other like he'd done. Suddenly I felt hot, as though the blood had rushed up to the skin everywhere and sweat broke out on my scalp—and at the same time I felt so incredibly horny.

"Fuck me," he whispered. "But go slow at first. I'm not used to guys your size, and you are so fucking big."

All I wanted to do right then and there was shove my cock as far inside of him as it would go. I wanted to touch him everywhere. I wanted to make him feel as incredible as I did, but I did as he asked. I found the opening down there with the head of my cock, and slowly started to work it in. He gasped a little at first, and resisted, but as I worked my way in, his head went back and his eyes closed.

I was about halfway in when he put his hand against my chest to stop me. He inhaled from the bottle again and handed it to me. I inhaled, and as I put the cap back on the bottle I felt him completely relax.

I went all the way in.

His head went back and his mouth opened. "Oh . . . my . . . God . . ."

I started moving back and forth, pulling my cock all the

way except for the head before shoving it in as far as I could.

"Oh . . . God . . . yes . . . fuck . . . me . . . .Jeff, please . . ."

I started going faster.

His eyes rolled back into his head, and he let out a loud grunt with each penetration.

I could feel it starting within me.

I pounded deeper and faster and harder.

He screamed as come flew out of his cock, his head lolling about as I felt mine go. My entire body stiffened. I was moaning, making noises like an animal as I shot my own load.

We both convulsed, our bodies shaking.

And then it was over.

He opened his eyes and smiled at me.

I leaned down and kissed him.

He peeled the condom off me and wiped himself down with a towel, which he tossed to the floor.

"I want to sleep with your arms around me," he whispered.

We snuggled down into the big bed, his ass against my crotch and my arms around him. I buried my head in the back of his neck.

He was asleep in an instant.

I love you, Blair, I mouthed soundlessly to the back of his head.

And before long, I too, fell asleep.

PART TWO

FALL

Chapter 6

"I expect you to kick his ass, you know," Blair said, putting his arm around my bare shoulders.

"You know it. Piece of cake." I grinned down at him while trying to stay standing. In fact, I wasn't sure if I could stand up if I didn't have my arm around his shoulder. I didn't know how I could possibly wrestle, as drunk as I was, but was going to give it my best shot. I didn't want to let Blair down.

Big Brother Night for Beta Kappa is four weeks into the pledging semester. The second week of school is always Rush Week, but I got my pledge bid on the very first night. Marc Kearney, the pledge master, a nice looking twenty-year-old junior with a thick brown mustache, took me into the president's office, where I sat in a chair and was asked if I wanted a pledge bid. I grinned and said, "yes," and one of the proudest moments of my life thus far was switching my nametag from JEFF MORGAN—GUEST proudly to JEFF MORGAN—PLEDGE within an hour of my arrival that Monday night. That following Saturday night was the pinning ceremony. My eleven fellow pledges and I swore an oath to do our best and never embarrass the Brotherhood, and then we were given our pledge pins, manuals, and our little black books. We were required to wear the pin at all times, unless sleeping or in the shower, until we made it through the semester—likewise, the black book had to always be handy. A brother had the right to ask me for it at any time, and if I couldn't produce it, it was a strike. Three strikes and you could be depledged. And that was the last thing in the world I wanted to have happen.

I'd fallen in love with being a brother of Beta Kappa. It was more than just being in love with Blair—although that certainly didn't hurt. It was the first place I ever felt like I *belonged*, even though I didn't officially yet. Even though I'd been accepted at Southern Heights, even being Homecoming King my senior year, I never really felt like I'd belonged there, and I certainly didn't feel that way after we'd moved to Polk. Everything about Polk still seemed alien to me—except for Beta Kappa. All the brothers seemed to be cool, the lessons we had to learn from the manual every week didn't seem hard (the Greek alphabet, the creed of the fraternity, etc.) and even when they lined us up for what they called *Hearth* (we stood in what they called the Great Room—the big room in the front where we had parties and also served as a dining hall—on the ledge with the fireplace, they dimmed the lights, and we answered questions and recited our weekly lessons) it didn't seem so bad. There were all kinds of games, too. The purpose of the black book was to help us learn who all the brothers were—we had to get their names, home addresses, majors, and pledge semester recorded in there. They were also allowed to give us up to three assignments—within reason; anything that seemed out of line we were supposed to bring to the pledge master for his decision.

There was also a thing called *bagging*—two brothers or two little sisters, at any time, could "bag" a pledge—kidnap him and hang out with him for the evening. So far, I'd been bagged once—by Jerry Pollard and another brother named Chris Morales—and all they did was drag me back to Chris's off-campus apartment, get me incredibly drunk and stoned, and we hung out while listening to the Grateful Dead.

It was *awesome.*

And for the most part, I liked my eleven pledge brothers.

Beta Kappa was the best thing that ever happened to me. My parents were also excited about it. They'd gotten married right out of high school, and Mom had worked while Dad went to college. Dad confessed to me, after I proudly showed him my pledge pin, that even though he loved Mom and loved being married to her, his biggest regret was not being able to fully live the college experience—and he was glad I was getting to. They gladly paid my pledge fees—and still no mention of me having to get a job.

And I sure as hell wasn't going to get one until I had to— I was having too much fun in my free time.

I'd really become fond of beer and pot.

Big Brother Night had begun with all twelve of us pledges meeting under the basketball post at the end of the parking lot. The house was dark and completely closed off; no one could see in or out. My eleven pledge brothers all seemed cool so far—my favorites were two guys my own age; Chris Moore and Eric Matthews. They were from Sonora, up in the mountains, and had apparently been friends since the cradle. Chris was taller than me, about six four, with dirty blond hair and gray eyes. He had a great body, as well. Eric was about my height, with dark hair and brown eyes. They were great guys, always joking and laughing. And when we lined up as a pledge class, we lined up alphabetically, so it was Eric, Chris, and then me. The guy who always stood to my right was Ted Norris, a junior majoring in Biology with an acne problem as well as a soft, flabby body. Ted was the odd man out in the pledge class. He was a loudmouth, and liked to brag—and he frankly got on my nerves. He was also a complainer. When Chris beat him out for pledge president, (unanimously, I might add) he'd asked for a recount. Everyone thought he was joking, but I could tell by the look in his eyes he wasn't. He also had trouble learning his lessons every week; we could count on him to choke and blow it on Hearth, no matter how much we worked with him beforehand.

I doubted he'd make it through the pledge semester.

My other pledge brothers (our first lesson had been to memorize their names, year in school, majors, and home-towns) were:

Tommy Amundsen, a sophomore from Mission Viejo, was a short redhead who maybe weighed about one hundred and twenty pounds on a heavy day. He was majoring in Political Science, and was relatively quiet. He had a great sense of humor though, and would be sitting there quietly when all of a sudden he would just say the funniest damned thing that would crack us all up. He had a longtime girl-friend, Jan, who was pledging over at Delta Zeta.

Steve Bradley was a junior from Boston who said "caaaah" instead of car and was majoring in Environmental Studies. He was just under six feet tall with curly bluish black hair, brown eyes so dark they were almost black, and a big smile with large white teeth. He had started lifting weights as an early teen after he'd been hospitalized and gone through extensive physical therapy after a car accident ("I had to learn how to walk again," he'd told us all solemnly at our "get-acquainted" meeting, "and I realized how important it is to be in good physical condition.") He was always drinking protein shakes and there were always a couple of protein bars in his backpack. He worked part-time as a personal trainer at Polk Fitness, and offered to design programs for all of us for free.

Brad Cassidy, a sophomore from Walnut Grove in the Bay Area, was majoring in Pre-Law and was also in the campus ROTC. He was only about five seven, and because of ROTC his hair was clipped close to his scalp. He also wore a mustache and a goatee. While he was capable of relaxing and having a good time, most of the time he was deadly serious about his plans to become a civil rights attorney.

Michael Durkiewicz was from Chicago, with pale white skin, light blue eyes, and sandy brown hair. He was about my height, and had been a lineman on his football team in high school. He was a big boy, probably topping the scales at around two hundred forty pounds. He was majoring in Physical Therapy and was always joking about getting "his fat ass in better shape," but he ate like a horse and was always hungry.

Cade Fontenot was something else entirely. Cade was of pure Cajun descent from just outside New Orleans, and Cade loved to have a good time. He was a sophomore majoring in Computer Science, and was only about five five, but he'd been a wrestler in his high school ("finished third in the state both my junior and senior years" he often said proudly) and so he had a thickly muscled, well-defined body to go with his dark hair, green eyes, and olive skin. Cade was always the first to suggest that we either get drunk or stoned—or preferably, both.

Joe Garza was Hispanic and from San Diego, a freshman majoring in Business. Joe was another one who liked to have fun, was about five ten, and dark. He always wore sandals, was always lugging his guitar around with him, and would start playing and singing at the merest suggestion he entertain us all. He was a good player and had a good voice, and once confided to me when he was stoned that he "really wanted to be a recording artist," but his parents were making him major in Business as a backup. We bonded over that, since my parents were the same way about my writing.

Rob Ross was a senior majoring in Psychology, was on the Dean's List, and had already been accepted into the graduate program. He was a nice looking guy with blond hair and brown eyes from Cleveland, and was engaged to one of the sisters of Alpha Xi Delta—Carrie Drilling (which, of course, led to the joke "Wouldn't you rather be drilling Carrie?").

The last of my pledge brothers was Jason Ziebell from Madison, Wisconsin. While I had really bonded with Chris and Eric (and felt attracted to them in a way), if I hadn't been already involved with Blair, Jason would be the one that I would want. He grew up ice skating and playing hockey, and as such had the roundest, thickest, hardest ass I'd ever seen in my life. You couldn't help but notice it, especially since even in the baggiest shorts it was prominent. He was in good shape everywhere, but that ass—and his legs—were the things fantasies came from. Jason had bright blue eyes, light skin, thick lips, and curly reddish gold hair. When he smiled, he lit up the room. Jason was majoring in History and was a little on the shy side. But when he opened up, he had a great sense of humor and was sharp as a tack.

After we had lined up, Marc Kearney came out and took

our car keys. "Welcome to Big Brother night," he said solemnly once he had placed our keys into a backpack. "Thus far,
your pledging semester has been easy and fun. But starting
tonight, it is going to get harder. So, to assist you, you are
getting your big brothers tonight. Your big brother will help
guide you through the semester. He will be your friend,
your mentor, and your ally in Beta Kappa." He then flashed
his teeth in a smile. "In a single file line, follow me now into
the house."

We followed him into the Great Room, where he had us
line up against the wall. All the brothers were gathered in a
crowd, watching us file in. "Turn and face the wall," Marc
instructed, and we did. "Now, you will be blindfolded."
Someone came up behind me and tied something around
my head, completely blocking my eyes. "Your big brother is
standing behind you. He is going to put something in your
hands. This is your house family beer. When your big
brothers were pledges and got THEIR big brothers, they
were given this beer to drink—going all the way back to the
founding of Beta Kappa. You have to drink it as quickly as
you can. You have to drink it all, pledges. And when you are
done, you will place it upside down on top of your head to
show us that you are finished. When you are all finished
with your family beer, then and only then will you be per-
mitted to find out who your big brother is."

A cold bottle was placed in my hands.

"Start drinking!" Marc instructed, and I raised the bottle
to my lips as all the brothers started shouting. The bottle
seemed bottomless, and I couldn't really taste whatever it
was I was drinking. I just kept swallowing and trying to
breathe through my nose. It seemed liked people were
screaming at me from every direction, but I knew that wasn't

possible. I just kept drinking and drinking until suddenly my stomach rebelled, and I leaned my head against the wall.

"YOU AREN'T FINISHED DRINKING, PLEDGE! THAT BOTTLE IS NOT EMPTY!" someone screamed in my right ear.

I lifted the bottle to my lips again, took a deep breath, and started drinking again. Whatever it was, it tasted absolutely horrible. My stomach kept trying to send whatever it was I was drinking back up but I kept fighting it down. *Just finish it, just finish it and then you can throw it up if you have to, just keep drinking . . .*

"Just turn it upside down on your head," a voice I didn't recognize whispered in my left ear. "You don't have to finish it—just as long as the bottle is empty."

With a sigh of relief, I did, and some liquid poured down over my head, dripping down my neck and soaking my shirt.

I stood there, panting, fighting down the urge to let it all come back up.

I felt woozy and sick.

After a few more minutes passed, minutes that seemed to last an eternity, the shouting finally stopped, and in the silence, Marc said, "Okay, pledges. Nicely done. Now you may remove your blindfolds and turn around. The first face you see will be your big brother."

I reached up and pulled the blindfold up. I looked at my hand. There was a liter bottle of Olde English 800 in it. I turned around and Blair was smiling at me.

Delighted, I threw my arms around him. "But I thought you said—"

"Just fucking with you," he whispered in my ear. "I wanted it to be a surprise."

The previous Monday night we'd made our lists for our choices for big brothers. Blair had told me over and over again that they probably wouldn't let me have him, even if I picked him, because everyone knew we were already close. I picked him as my first choice anyway, and hoped. I also listed Rory, Marc, Jerry Pollard, and Chris Morales.

But I really didn't want anyone besides Blair.

"I'll try to take care of you tonight," he whispered, "but I can't promise anything."

"What do you mean?" I stared at him. That had a rather ominous tone to it I wasn't quite comfortable with. What did they have in store for us?

He just shook his head as Marc blew a whistle and the room quieted again. "Look at you pledges," Marc walked along the line of us, "you're all a mess. A disgrace to the name of Beta Kappa! Beta Kappas don't waste beer, you know, and every single one of you is wearing your family beer. You were supposed to drink it, not fucking wear it. Tsk, tsk, tsk. What are we going to do with these pledges?"

"It's a disgrace!" someone shouted, and other brothers began murmuring agreement.

Marc turned to the crowd of brothers. I looked at Blair, and he closed his right eye in a wink. "What should we do with these sloppy pledges?"

"Get them out of those clothes!" someone shouted.

The crowd cheered, and I looked over at Blair, who just shrugged his shoulders and gave me a sheepish grin. Marc blew the whistle again, and everyone fell silent. "You heard the brothers, pledges. Get out of those clothes," he said quietly.

Chris and I looked at each other, our eyes wide.

Are they serious?

Marc blew the whistle again. "Did I speak in a fucking foreign language? I SAID GET OUT OF THOSE CLOTHES!" he screamed at us.

The brothers started chanting, "STRIP! STRIP! STRIP!" and clapping in unison.

I looked at Blair, and he made a face as he nodded. I started unbuttoning my shirt. The brothers kept chanting. Blair and the other big brothers walked up to their little brothers and stood in front of us. "Give me your clothes," Blair said over the chanting. "I'll put 'em in my room. Don't want you to lose them. That's happened before."

I handed him my shirt and took off my shoes and socks. "Why do we have to get undressed?"

"It's just part of the ritual of the night," Blair said. "It won't be the last time you're in your underwear in front of the Brotherhood."

"Um—" *What the hell does that mean?*

"Relax," he whispered, "it's no worse than wearing that bikini at that pool party we had, remember? And at least no one here is going to be judging your body."

I undid my pants and pulled them off, handing them to Blair, who folded them. All around me my pledge brothers were fumbling to get out of their clothes. I felt drunk from the Olde English 800; at one point I leaned back against the wall to maintain my balance. The brothers were still all screaming. Ted Norris fell down when pulling his pants off, and I looked at him with more than a little disgust. His body was even worse unclothed than I could have imagined. He had tits, for God's sake, and it looked like his skin had never been exposed to the sun. He had this stricken look on his face, and his big brother—a tall, good-looking guy from Oregon named Dave Pittenger—looked just as disgusted as I felt. Ted was constantly bragging at pledge meetings about being a star jock in high school, how popular he'd been, and how many "chicks" he'd bagged. *How was that possible*, I wondered, looking at his soft flabby body. *He doesn't look like he's ever done any kind of exercise his entire life. What is wrong with him? Why does he lie all the time? Why can't he just be himself and stop trying to impress everyone?*

Not for the first time, I wished he would drop out of the pledge class.

Marc blew the whistle again, and the crowd of brothers moved back again. Marc walked along the line of us, looking us up and down. When he reached the end of the lineup, he walked back along, this time shaking his head. He walked out in front of us. "All right, pledges, do you know what I see when I look at you? I see a bunch of clay that needs to be remolded into brothers of Beta Kappa. You've had it pretty easy so far this semester, but from now on it's going to be a lot harder. We need to find out if each and every one of you has what it takes. You are a unit. If one of you fails, all of you fail. You have to help each other out. A chain is only as strong as its weakest link—and likewise, your unit is only as strong as its weakest link. Do you understand me?"

"SIR! YES SIR!" we shouted back in unison. They'd taught us that—they called it the "sir" sandwich; if we were ever addressed by the name *pledge*, we had to start each sentence with sir as well as finish it that way. It was kind of like being in the military in a way; I'd commented about this once to Blair. Blair shrugged, "I think it comes from the after World War II period, when everyone was in college on the GI Bill. They joined fraternities and brought the whole military thing with them."

I glanced at Ted out of the corner of my eye. He was going to be the weak link in our chain, there was no question about that in my mind.

"Good." Marc replied. "Now, it's game time. Pledges vs. their Big Brothers. Are you ready to compete, pledges?"

"SIR! YES SIR!"

"All right. Let the games begin." He smiled. "And don't embarrass me too badly, pledges. You know your performance reflects on me. Don't let me down."

The first game was called *beer relay*. Two troughs of beer were set up, and the pledged lined up alongside their big brothers. When Marc blew a whistle, the pair at the front of the lines had to run to the trough, stick their face in it, and drink as much as they could for a minute, when Marc would blow the whistle again. Those two went to the back of the line and the next two took their turn. Whichever trough emptied first signified the winning team, while the rest of the brothers stood around with cups of beer cheering on the brothers—jeering and mocking us.

I didn't know how I could possibly drink any more beer after chugging down that huge bottle, but the other pledges were in the same boat as I was. Actually, some of them looked worse off than me. Jason Ziebell looked positively green. His curly reddish gold hair was soaked through and plastered to the side of his head. He was either going to puke or pass out at any second. I couldn't help but look at his ass, though. His white underwear was soaked through and clung to him like plastic wrap.

And Ted looked like he was going to blow chunks at any minute. He was leaning on Dave Pittenger, who looked like he wished he were anywhere else but there. Even Chris and Eric, who took great pride in how much they could drink, looked glassy eyed. All of my pledge brothers looked the worse for wear, and when Marc blew the whistle the first time and Tommy staggered to the trough and stuck his face in the big puddle of beer, I worried he might not be able to get back up again. Tommy was a lightweight when it came to drinking—one beer made him drunk, two and he was a complete mess—so I wasn't sure how long he would last. Sure enough, once the whistle blew again, Tommy couldn't get up. His big brother, Chris Morales, had to help him to his feet, and even then he couldn't straighten up. Chris walked him to the back of the line, where he passed Tommy off to Jason—which was kind of like propping up a sand castle with water. I just kept taking deep breaths. My stomach was lurching, and I knew it was just going to be a matter of time before all that beer was coming back up. Every so often Blair and I would make eye contact, and he would give me a reassuring smile as we moved closer to the front of the lines.

When it was finally my turn, Blair and I raced up to the trough. It was obvious the brothers were going to finish their trough long before we were, but I gamely stuck my head down into the beer, gulping down as much as I could stand despite the turmoil in my stomach. When the whistle blew again, it took me a lot longer to run back to the end of the line than it should have—and I almost fell down once or twice. Chris Moore stepped up and helped me to the back of the line, both of us weaving. "Thanks, man," I breathed out, bending at the waist and taking some deep breaths. Everything was kind of spinning in my head, and I was having trouble focusing. Chris smacked me on the back.

"You okay?" Blair asked. He was standing next to me, kneeling so our faces were at the same level.

I just nodded, letting out a huge belch that tasted like beer.

He shook his head and smiled. "Hang in there, Jeff. This should be over soon."

My second time at the trough, I really didn't think I was going to be able to get back up again. When I got to my feet, everything seemed out of focus, and the room did really start spinning. Suddenly I could feel all the beer starting to come back up . . . and my entire body seemed to heave. I fought it down, but my stomach fought back.

"HE'S GONNA PUKE!" someone shouted, and through the haze I realized they were talking about me.

"Get to the bathroom, pledge!"

"Don't you dare blow chunks in the Great Room!"

"Puke! Puke! Puke!"

I realized the race had been paused, and all the brothers were chanting "Puke!" at me. Every eye in the room was focused on me, and as I looked around the room, my body still trying to reject the beer out my mouth, I saw the delight on the faces of not only the brothers but my fellow pledges—every single one of them wanted to throw up as well, but didn't want to be the first. Once one of us puked, the rest of them would follow suit—but no one wanted the disgrace of being the first.

And then my gaze locked with Blair's.

He shook his head slightly "no."

I looked around at the other faces.

I looked back at Blair and smiled.

No fucking way was I going to be the first. No way was I going to puke before Tommy or Ted. Uh-uh, no way. Not going to happen.

From somewhere, I summoned the will to keep the beer down.

I turned to face the brothers and bowed my head slightly. "Not me!" I shouted as I got my stomach under control. "IT WON'T BE ME!" My stomach seemed to settle, and I raised my hands over my head like a boxer who's just knocked out his opponent. "More beer! Bring me more beer!"

Man, was I drunk.

The brothers let out a cheer.

And just as I shouted the words, Ted Norris made a gagging noise and a stream of foamy beer launched out of his mouth on to the floor. He fell to his hands and knees, and even after everything had stopped coming up, he had the dry heaves. Dave Pittenger just shook his head and went for a mop. He slapped the mop handle down in front of Ted. "When you're done, you can mop up that mess." Dave stood up rolling his eyes, and walked over to the keg.

Blair smiled at me proudly, and the relay started up again like it had never stopped.

I only had one more turn at the trough before the brothers won. Instead of drinking, I just stuck my face down there and pretended to swallow while breathing through my nose—but the smell of the beer didn't help my stomach any. It was all over me, and my fingers were even beginning to wrinkle. My hair reeked of beer and was completely soaked. Once the brothers were pronounced the winners, drinking games started up at the tables set up throughout the Great Room—Mexicali, Quarters, Cardinal Puff, every conceivable drinking game was going on, including some I'd never heard of. Blair grabbed me. "Come on, let's get you out of here for a minute," he said, and steered me to his room, shutting and locking the door behind us.

"Little bro," he said, throwing his arms around me. I put mine around him and picked him up, hugging him hard in my drunken stupor. "You're hurting me!" he laughed, pushing me away. "Let me down, you big drunk prairie boy!"

I put him down and sat down on the bed. "I'm so wasted." I looked up at him in wonder. The posters on his wall were all blurry. "Oooohhhh—I don't think I've ever been this drunk. Ever." The room began to spin a bit, and I closed my eyes. *Deep breaths, take lots of deep breaths.*

"Well, if you need to puke, make sure the coast is clear and do it out the window into the bushes." Blair replied, getting the dragon out and loading the bowl. "You know they keep track of every pledge who pukes and write it on the chalkboard. The goal is for every pledge to puke—but I wanted you to take a break from the drinking for a while, spend some quality time with your big brother, and get a little stoned. Besides, all the games are rigged, if you didn't notice. You boys are outnumbered, and the brothers are going to gang up on you all until you puke." He grinned at me. "Besides, you need to be ready for pledge wrestling later."

"Pledge wrestling? What's that?"

He handed me the dragon. "Around midnight, the pledges who haven't puked yet are gathered in the Great Room, drenched in beer and have to wrestle each other." He shook his head. "Wrestling will make you puke, trust me. Any pledge who makes it through the night without puking earns the respect of the brotherhood though—especially since the whole purpose of the night is to make the pledges puke." He inclined his head toward the window. "So, you might want to go ahead and do it now—in secret—so later when it comes to the wrestling, not only will you not puke, you'll win." He grinned at me. "Sure, it's cheating, but who cares? I want everyone to be jealous of my little brother."

The room started spinning again when I sat up. Nausea swept over me, and I felt hot. "Maybe . . . I . . . should . . ."

Blair walked over to the window and looked out. He slid the window open. "Go for it."

I stuck my head out the window, opened my mouth, and a stream of foamy beer spewed out. I wiped my mouth with my hand, and immediately felt a lot better. I turned around and said, "Thanks, Blair." I sat down again on the bed.

"What are big brothers for?" He sat down at his desk and took a hit off the bong.

We got stoned and cuddled for a little while, and then he said we needed to get back to the Great Room. As we passed the chalkboard, I noticed that every pledge's name was up there except mine and Eric's. "Hmmm," Blair said, looking at the board. "Looks like you and Eric might be wrestling. Unless, of course we can make Eric puke before midnight."

I winked at him. "Sounds like a plan."

We walked back into the Great Room, and joined a game of Quarters that Eric and his big brother, Marc Kearney, were also playing. It didn't take long to figure out what was going on. Every time a brother got a quarter in the cup, either Eric or I had to drink. Eric was looking pretty drunk. I was buzzing pretty hard myself, but since I'd puked up most of the beer I'd already drunk, it was mostly from the pot, so being forced to drink during the game wasn't bothering me. I kept looking at Eric. Every time I made a quarter in the cup, I made Eric drink. The brothers, though, soon figured out what I was up to, so they started ganging up on me. Eric was hopeless. Whenever it was his turn to bounce the quarter, it didn't even come remotely close to going into the cup.

His eyelids were drooping, and even though he was sitting down, he was weaving from side to side. His usually curly hair was drenched in beer and plastered to the side of his head. The hair on his chest was also wet and stuck to his skin. He had a nice tan, and an even nicer body. His shoulders were broad, his chest and arms thickly muscled. His waist was narrow and his stomach flat. His white underwear was also soaked through, and I could see the dark pubic hair and his thick cock and balls clearly. He was hot, and he looked strong. If we had to wrestle sometime with him sober, he'd probably wipe the floor with me. Drunk as he was, though, I could probably take him if it came down to that.

And it did. Somehow, he made it through another half hour of the game without either passing out or throwing up.

He'd just taken another drink when Marc suddenly stood up and blew the whistle. All sound ceased, and everyone turned to look at him. He climbed up on his chair. He was pretty drunk himself, and I looked at Blair, who winked. "Brothers!" Marc shouted. He was weaving on the chair, and looked like he might fall off any minute. "We have two pledges left who have not yet tossed their cookies. You know what that means?"

"PLEDGE WRESTLING!" someone shouted in response, and everyone cheered.

Blair leaned over to me, "Okay, little bro, are you ready for this?"

"I think so." I put my hands down on the table and pushed myself up. I wobbled a little bit once I was on my feet, but at least I was able to get up by myself. Two brothers had to help Eric up, and even then they had to stay with him.

That was a very good sign.

Some brothers moved the sofas off the carpeted area in the Great Room, leaving a big clearing. Some brothers jumped up on the hearth, and all the others crowded around. A couple of other brothers spread a tarp over the rug, and then beer was dumped all over me—as if I wasn't already soaked in it. Out of the corner of my eye I could see Eric being similarly drenched. "Just remember," Blair whispered, "whenever you can, try to squeeze his stomach. If you can, land on it. He'll puke, you'll be the winner, and that's the end of it."

"Okay," I replied, leaning on him heavily.

"I expect you to kick his ass."

"Piece of cake," I replied. Drunk as I was, at least I had a plan. I wasn't sure if Eric could even think, or even knew what was going on.

"Pledges to the center of the tarp!" Marc announced. Eric and I walked out there and stood on either side of him. "Okay, the rules of pledge wrestling is you keep wrestling until one or both of you puke. Whoever pukes last is the winner."

"We don't try for a pin?" Eric slurred. I looked at him. His eyes were half shut, and he was having trouble keeping his balance. He was swaying from side to side, and every once in a while would sway so far to one side he'd stumble a bit until he got his balance again. I was pretty wasted my-

self, but I was a lot better off than he was. *Thank you, Blair,*
for taking me to your room.

"Pins?" Marc laughed. "Stupid, stupid pledge! We don't
care if someone gets pinned! WHAT DO WE CARE
ABOUT, BROTHERS?"

"PUKE! PUKE! PUKE!" they started chanting again.

Over the noise, Marc said to both of us, "Now, no punch-
ing, biting, scratching, anything like that. When I blow this
whistle, you start wrestling. Got it?"

"Uh-huh," I replied.

"Eric?"

"Sure." He was weaving even worse than he had been. I
didn't even think he knew where he was.

Marc stepped up on the hearth and blew the whistle.

I turned. Eric hadn't moved. I looked over at Blair and
shrugged. I walked over to Eric and gave him a good, hard
shove. He toppled over, and hit the floor with a bone-
wrenching thud. The brothers were still chanting. I walked
over to where Eric was lying on the tarp. He grinned up at
me, and I sat down hard on his stomach. His eyes got wide,
and I felt his stomach starting to retch, so I bounced on it
one more time, and I saw it coming. I got up quickly and
moved back over to the sidelines, and Eric rolled over onto
his stomach and puked.

"We have a winner!" Marc shouted, and Blair raised my
hand in triumph.

The brothers cheered me, and crowded around me. "A
victory beer!" Jerry Pollard said, shoving a full cup into my
hand. As I raised it to my lips, everyone started chanting,
"Chug! Chug! Chug!"

So, I did.

And when the cup was empty, I put it on top of my head upside down.

And then everything in my stomach came up in a rush.

That's the last thing I remember about Big Brother Night, other than waking up in Blair's arms the next morning . . .

Chapter 7

Little Sister Rush was the week after Big Brother night. Since pledge rush was an officially sanctioned university event, the university had decreed sometime during the Reagan years that no liquor could be served to pledges. I couldn't imagine what it must have been like when Rush Week wasn't dry. Blair told me that one of the alumni said "we used to put pledge pins on the unconscious ones—and they couldn't remember if they'd actually said yes or not."

Needless to say, the size of Beta Kappa pledge classes declined after Rush Week went dry.

So, Little Sister Rush, which was unofficial, was planned to more than make up for the sobriety of Rush Week. "The whole point," Blair explained to me that Wednesday night, before the first party started officially, "is to see which girls can party really hard as well as will put out for the brotherhood."

"Um, that's kind of disgusting." I replied, passing the dragon back to him. "And degrading."

Blair shrugged. "I agree with you—but then, the girls allow themselves to be degraded—and nobody forces them to get drunk. I told you how the straight boys are—they don't care who gets them off as long as they get off. You wouldn't believe some of the pigs I've seen guys with— blech."

"I don't know, it sounds to me like a perfect setup for a date rape accusation." I put the bong down.

"Yeah, I've wondered about that." He shrugged. "You'd think with all the drunk girls putting out at parties all the time on Fraternity Row, that would happen a lot more. Go figure."

That first night's party wasn't much fun, it turned out. Maybe because it was on a Wednesday night, with two more school days to get through. The Brotherhood didn't put a lot of effort into it. It was held in the Great Room, and the party's theme was a rather lame one, I thought: *Behind the Mask*. Everyone got a cheap mask to put over their eyes when they walked in—pledges took turns working the desk handing out the masks—and we were supposed to wear them all night. Blair of course had a fabulous mask from New Orleans Mardi Gras; an amazing contraption made to look like real gold and covered in glitter with peacock feathers sticking out of it. There was a keg of beer set up in the Great Room, and again, we pledges took turns filling up people's cups with beer. Someone had put on a couple of dance mix CD's on shuffle on the stereo, and everyone just kind of lounged around and chatted. It was boring as hell, and hardly anyone showed up for it except for sorority girls looking for a free drunk, apparently. "I hate those girls," Marc Kearney said to Jason Ziebell and me while we were on keg duty. "They come to Little Sister Rush every year and never join up. They just like to drink our booze, the whores."

Thursday night was different, though. That was International Drink Night, and the entire party was held in the second floor hallway. Every room on the second floor hosted a separate drink—and there were fifteen rooms up there. So, basically, there was a party going on in every room. Stereos were blasting competing music—everything from hip hop to rap to hard rock to techno. My personal favorite was the upside-down margaritas—you sat down in a chair, put your head back, and someone poured tequila in your mouth from one side while someone poured margarita mix in from the other side. Once your mouth was full of liquid, you closed your mouth and they shook your head to "mix" the drink before you swallowed. I had three of those, as well as a couple of Come-In-A-Hot-Tubs, and a few depth charges (a shot glass full of whiskey dropped into a mug of beer, which you then had to chug down), and was pretty much feeling no pain the majority of the evening. The upstairs was packed full of loud, drunk people within twenty minutes of the party starting. I drank way too much—as usual—and wound up spending the night passed out in Blair's bed.

But I don't think I puked.

It wasn't as easy for Blair and I to be together as I would have liked. There were always people around once school started and everyone came back to live in the house. It seemed like all we were doing was stealing time together—having to wait until whoever stopped by his room with a couple of joints and a twelve-pack of beer were fucked up enough to finally go away and leave us alone. Sometimes I just got tired of waiting and would go on home, to lie in my bed and remember the times we were together while I jacked off. It was incredibly frustrating—especially because I didn't have anyone I could talk to about my feelings for

Blair. I was in love with him. I wanted nothing more than to spend my every minute with him. But I didn't know how Blair felt about me . . . I knew he cared, but did he love me as a friend with benefits or was he in love with me? I wasn't sure of anything anymore. So many times after I'd fucked him and we lay in each other's arms, I wanted to say *I love you*, but I could never forget the time I'd said it and how he'd reacted. I wanted him to say the words to me so badly, but somehow I knew it was never going to happen. And in the silent loneliness of my bedroom, sometimes I cried.

Friday night I pulled into the parking lot of the house at six-thirty. I had a late Biology lab every Friday afternoon, which saved me from the pledge duty of being at the house early to help set up parties. The fraternity's motto was *Alma mater first, and Beta Kappa for alma mater*—in other words, school comes first—so no one other than Ted Norris ever complained about me not being able to help out before the parties. It was pretty obvious that my pledge brothers were getting just as exasperated over Ted as I already was. I didn't think he was going to make it through the semester. When he wasn't around, all of us complained and bitched about him. Chris tried talking to him once about his attitude, and got told to fuck off for his trouble. The brothers picked on him mercilessly, and the assignments he got in his black book were much more difficult than the ones the rest of us got—in fact, the vast majority of mine were *Bag me sometime! I'll pay for the beer.* Sometimes I felt sorry for Ted; but then he would do or say something that would remind me just exactly why I didn't like him in the first place.

As I walked up to the house, my jaw dropped. The Friday night theme was Mai Tai Wun On, which apparently was a long-standing house tradition. When the brothers talked about how they turned the house into a Polynesian paradise for this annual party, I rolled my eyes inwardly. I mean, really, how convincing could any decoration be? And the Behind the Mask party on Wednesday night had been pretty fucking lame after all. But now, I couldn't believe my eyes. I just stared in wonder. The entire backyard was covered by a blue tarp, wrapped around railroad ties, which made up a lagoon. Tiki torches lined the sidewalk. A waterfall off the roof splashed into the lagoon, and inside the lagoon itself several fountains shot streams of water up into the air. Flower petals floated in the water, as well as tea candles floating in salad bowls wrapped in tin foil. That side of the house was completely covered in palm fronds. The front door stood open, and inside I could see a huge papier-mâché tiki god with a mai tai fountain inside his mouth. I was completely blown away. How had they managed to do this so quickly? In just one day?

I felt very proud to be a Beta Kappa pledge. We were sooo the coolest house on campus.

I walked in the front door, and the first thing I heard was Ted's nasal voice, "About fucking time you got here, Morgan."

"Shut up, Ted," Chris Moore snapped. He was struggling to tap a keg. "Good to see you, Jeff. I've got your shirt."

Every year, the house specially made T-shirts for the party. This year's design was a dark blue shirt with the Beta Kappa letters transposed over a scene of a girl in a bikini coming out of a tropical lagoon—I think it was actually an image ripped off from a *Sports Illustrated* swimsuit issue. I pulled off my shirt and folded it, putting it inside my backpack. Chris tossed me my party T-shirt, which I pulled on over my head. It was tight and hugged my upper body like a glove. "What needs to be done?"

"Everything's done already, as usual," Ted sneered. "As always, you just showed up in time for the party."

"You know, Ted, maybe if you focused on what you need to do instead of what everyone else is doing, you wouldn't forget your lessons on Hearth," Chris snapped before I had a chance to say anything. What I wanted to do was punch Ted in the mouth, and I could feel my face flush. Instead, I counted to ten.

The previous Monday, every single time Ted had been called on, he hadn't been able to recite any lesson requested of him, to the murmurs of a disgusted Brotherhood. He even fucked up the Greek alphabet, which was the easiest of all the lessons thus far. I could even say the damned thing backwards.

Ted flushed. "Yeah, well, fuck you, Moore." He snapped and stormed off.

"I didn't think he would ever go away," Chris said, rolling his eyes.

I laughed. "How can he not realize how abrasive he is?"

"It's beyond me. Unless he's an even bigger asshole than we think, and likes being one, I don't know." Chris shrugged. "I mean, I feel bad for him sometimes, but you know if he doesn't get his shit together we're all going to wind up suffering for it." He sighed. "You know, they keep telling us our class is only as strong as our weakest link—and he is definitely that."

"Word up." I changed the subject. "Where's Eric?"

"Oh, he had to run to the store for more mai tai mix. Can you believe how cool this place looks? This is fucking incredible."

"I know. I still can't believe it." I looked into the Great Room. All the walls were covered with palm fronds, and candles burned everywhere. The deejay was setting up his station by the carpeted area. "This party is going to be so awesome."

"You have no idea, little bro," Blair said from behind me. "Are you finished with the kegs, Pledge Moore?"

"Yes sir, Brother Blanchard sir." Chris straightened up with a big grin.

"Then I request the presence of you two pledges in my room." I turned around and started laughing. Blair was wearing the Mai Tai Wun On T-shirt, but had painted his face like a Polynesian headhunter, complete with a bone through his nose which I hoped was a clip-on, and was wearing a grass skirt underneath rather than pants. "What are you laughing at, little bro? I told you this party was a big deal." He waved. "Follow me, pledges."

Once we were inside his room, he locked the door and placed the obligatory towel across the bottom of the door. He walked over to his desk and got out the dragon. "I've heard through the brother grapevine, Chris, that you are a stoner. Did I hear correctly?"

"Sir, oh, yes, definitely sir." Chris grinned.

I plopped down on the bed. All the pledges—except Ted, of course—smoked pot. We got stoned at all of our pledge meetings. *Ted,* I thought as I waited for my turn with the dragon, *just doesn't fit in at all with the rest of us.* As far as I could tell, all the brothers, with a few exceptions, smoked pot too. For about the hundredth time since our first pledge meeting, I wondered why Ted had bothered pledging a fraternity—and why this one in particular.

After the dragon had gone around a few times, I could

hear the sound of voices outside as people started arriving for the party. Blair coughed. "I'm going to get us all a mai tai—you boys stay here, okay?"

"I can go." Chris said, blowing out a stream of smoke.

"No, I'll go. I want to hang out with you two for a while, and if you go out there someone might put you to work." Blair grabbed his keys and went out the door.

"He's so cool," Chris said, taking another hit. "You're so lucky he's your big brother."

"I think so, too." I took the dragon away from him.

"Man, I am stoned." He grinned at me. "Can I tell you a secret?"

"Sure man." I was pretty stoned myself. "You're my pledge brother. You can tell me anything."

"Man"—he leaned close to me and whispered—"it was so hot watching you and Eric wrestle last Saturday, even though it didn't last very long." He laughed. "Pretty smart of you to go for his stomach the way you did. Do you like to wrestle?"

"What?"

"Do you like to wrestle? I think it's sexy as hell—Eric loves doing it too. He was bummed he was too wasted to make a real match out of it, you know." He put a hand on my leg. "You've got an awesome body, guy. Eric wants to wrestle with you again. And so do I."

"Are you serious?" I felt myself starting to get hard. I remembered what it was like wrestling around with Kevin in high school, the feel of his muscles against mine, his legs wrapped around my head—and then I suppressed a laugh. I hadn't thought about Kevin since meeting Blair.

It was funny how things change.

He slid his hand up to my crotch. "Hell yeah, man. Why

don't you come by our apartment some time? We can get stoned, drink some beer, strip down, and get it on."

I licked my lips and considered. Chris and Eric were both sexy guys for sure. If not for what was going on between Blair and I, I probably would have crushes on both of them—and they would definitely play a part in my fantasies. Wrestling Eric had been fun—although I was relatively certain that sober he'd kick my ass. But then again, that could also be a lot of fun. But was it cheating on Blair? We'd never talked about not having sex with other people, and he had never said he loved me. Yeah, I loved him. I would probably always love him . . . but what would it hurt? And he'd never have to know. "Yeah, that would be fun, man."

Chris squeezed my crotch, and my dick got harder. "Awesome. Sooner rather than later, okay?"

The door opened and Blair walked in with three drinks. "Okay, what have you two been up to? You look guilty as hell." He kicked the door shut behind him.

Chris winked at me. "Just smoking your pot, sir."

Blair looked at both us, an eyebrow raised. "All right then." He handed over the drinks and sat down at his desk. "Place is getting crowded. Let's smoke a bit more, finish these, and join the party."

The party was amazing. The deejay was the same guy Beta Kappa used for all of its parties, and he knew how to get people dancing. I got hit on by a number of little sister prospectives, as well as some of the little sisters themselves. I flirted back with them, but when I didn't really respond as sexually as they obviously wanted, they moved on to other pledges or brothers. I had never really danced much before, but found myself getting pulled out on the dance floor over and over again. I kept an eye out for Blair—he was kind of hard to miss in that getup—but didn't see him as often as I would have liked, and whenever I did see him, by the time I could disentangle myself from whatever girl had latched onto me on the dance floor, he was gone. Every so often I would see Eric with some girl hanging on him, and would watch for a while. *So, wrestling me turned you on? So, what's the deal with the girl you're kissing right now?* And then one time, as I was thinking it and looking his body over, he looked over at me and smiled, then winked. He then turned his back to me, and started shaking his ass at me. To anyone else, it might have looked like he was just doing some kind of lame white-boy boogie step, but I knew exactly what he was doing. *He wants me to fuck him in the ass after we wrestle the next time.* And I felt my own dick getting hard as the Pussycat Dolls sang "Don't Cha".

And I kept dancing.

One time, I remember Chris dancing with some other nameless, faceless girl right next to me and the girl I was dancing with—I think her name was Dawn, or something like that, she was a longtime little sister and had a reputation for being quite the stoner—and he also started doing the white-boy boogie ass shaking thing before spinning around and winking at me, bursting into laughter.

He was sexy as hell. My dick stirred in my pants. *Oh yes, I am definitely going over to Chris and Eric's for some wrestling—sooner rather than later.*

And then I saw Ted Norris watching us both, his eyes narrowed.

When he saw me watching him, he turned around and stalked out of the Great Room.

Asshole, I thought, dismissing him from my mind.

The party finally started winding down around one in the morning. The floor of the Great Room was about an inch deep in beer and spilled mai tais. I was drenched in sweat, my legs ached from all the dancing, and I was quite drunk. I hadn't seen Blair in a long time, and since I was planning on spending the night in his room—way too drunk to drive home—I decided to go looking for him.

"You seen Blair?" I asked everyone I saw, but everyone shook their heads. I knocked on his door, but there was no answer.

"Dude. I think he went to Denny's with some people for breakfast," Rory Armagh said as he weaved by. He had his arm around a short blond girl with the largest tits I'd ever seen. "He'll be back in a while. Great party, huh?"

"Thanks, Rory." I called after him as he went into his room with the girl. *Well, I can go crash on a couch in the Great Room,* I thought, but decided to make a pass through the building before giving up on Blair entirely. It wasn't like him to take off like that and not tell me, and it bothered me more than a little bit. I walked down to the end of the hall and up the stairs to the second floor. As I walked past it, the door to room twenty opened and a girl came out in a hurry, almost knocking me down.

"Excuse me," she muttered and hurried down the hall and down the stairs.

Marc Kearney came out behind her, muttered a hello and rushed after her, but stopped at the top of the stairs. "Fuck." He turned back to me and gave me a sheepish grin. He was barefoot, and just wearing a pair of jeans. His lean torso was completely smooth other than a happy trail below his navel and the nest of hair under his arms. "So much for me getting some pussy tonight." He laughed. "What are you up to, Jeff?"

I shrugged. "Too drunk to drive home—supposed to stay in Blair's room, but can't find him."

"Ah, yes. A bunch of people went to Denny's, he was one of them I think." He clapped me on the shoulder. "You're welcome to hang out in here with me till he gets back. We've never really spent any time together."

"Thanks." I walked into his room and sat down on the bed. His walls were bare, and there was a smudged mirror out on his desk.

"Man, can you believe that whore led me on and then wouldn't put out?" Marc sat down in his desk chair and stretched. "She'd better not ever show her stupid face around here again, that's all I have to say. Cock teases aren't welcome here. You want a beer?"

"Sure," I replied, inwardly rolling my eyes. I sure hoped I wasn't going to have to listen to him talk about what a stud he was with girls until Blair got home. I wasn't sure why all the brothers seemed to feel the need to brag about that all the time, but all it convinced me of was it was all talk. There was one brother, though—Kevin Shaughnessy—who lived on the first floor who I especially didn't like. He was a junior active—just initiated the past spring—and drank like a fish and didn't know when to stop. He also was incredibly mean to the pledges. When totally fucked up, he had a tendency to strip naked and wander. And whenever he scored with a girl, he hung his stained sheets out his window to let every one know.

I couldn't stand him.

Marc got me a beer out of his little refrigerator and passed it to me. I popped the top and took a swig. "So, what do you think of Beta Kappa so far, Jeff?"

"I love it here, Marc. I'm really proud to be here."

"Good, good." He opened his desk drawer and got a folded piece of paper. He undid it, and scraped a small white rock out of it with a razor blade onto the mirror. "You want to do a line?"

"Um . . ." I hated showing my ignorance, but Jerry Pollard had told me the night he and Chris Morales bagged me *never do a drug offered to you without finding out what it is first.* "What is it?"

Marc let out his braying laugh. "Coke, my innocent little pledge. You've never tried it? Your nostrils are virgin territory?"

"Yeah." I grinned at him. "Everyone forgets I'm just a good ole prairie boy from Kansas. I was completely innocent until the Brotherhood corrupted me."

"Well, you seem to have taken a liking to corruption." He laughed and passed the mirror and the little straw over to me. I held it in one hand.

"What do I do?"

"You really are a virgin. Haven't you seen *Scarface?*" Marc laughed again, delighted with himself. "Just hold the mirror up high, hold the straw to your nostril, then inhale one of the lines, and keep inhaling until it's all gone."

I did as instructed, and when I was finished I handed the mirror and straw back to him. My entire right nostril went numb, and I had this weird taste in the back of my mouth. I gagged a bit, and then it felt like something slid down my throat. I grabbed my beer and took a swig as Marc laughed.

I took a deep breath, and my head suddenly went light. It felt like my entire body was floating, and I tried to grab the floor through my shoes with my toes to stay anchored. This was so absurd I started to giggle.

"Here." Marc ran his index finger over the mirror and

shoved it into my mouth, running it along my upper gum and then the lower. Both gums went instantly numb.

Without a second thought, I grabbed hold of his arm, not letting him pull his finger out of my mouth. Instead, I slid it between my teeth and started sucking on it.

I was suddenly, intensely horny.

"Well, what do we have here?" Marc asked, a smile playing over his face.

I smiled at him. "What do you want to have here?" I asked, still holding his arm.

He got out of his chair and walked over to where I sat on the bed, standing in between my legs. He leaned down and kissed me on the mouth. With my gums numb, it was a weird feeling—but one I really liked and definitely wanted to continue. He put his tongue in my mouth and I sucked on it. He moaned. I put my hands on his waist. His skin felt smooth, but hot, and as he leaned into me I moved my mouth down to his left nipple and licked it.

He put his head back. "Oh, man, that feels so good." He gasped, putting his hands on my head.

I undid the fly of his jeans, and pulled them down from his narrow hips. His dick was hard in his white underwear, and I put one hand on it. He moaned again, but pulled away from me. For a brief moment I was frightened, but he just smiled and turned his stereo on. REM filled the room with noise. "I kind of get loud, sometimes," he said with a sheepish grin. "And nobody needs to know what we're doing in here." He stepped out of his pants and tossed them on the floor.

I pulled my shirt off over my head.

"You have a beautiful chest," he said, sitting on my lap and putting his arms around my neck.

"You have a beautiful ass," I replied.

He kissed my neck, and his mustache tickled me a bit. He moved his mouth down from my neck to my nipples. "Your chest is so hot," he whispered, flicking his tongue out over first one nipple and then the other.

I moaned as my cock strained against my jeans. He reached down and felt my cock. His eyes opened wide. "That's big!"

"Yeah." I whispered back to him. "And it wants to be inside you. All the way."

He pushed me back onto the bed, and straddled my crotch. He ground his ass into my hard dick. "You wanna fuck me, prairie boy?"

"Uh-huh." I smiled up at him. "I want to fuck you till you scream."

"Mmmmm." He brought his mouth down to my nipples again and started working on them with his lips, teeth and tongue. I began to writhe and buck my hips up and down, dry humping his hot ass. He sat back up and smiled down at me. "Man, I want you inside me."

He got off me, and undid my jeans, pulling them down to my ankles, along with my underwear. My cock sprang free and smacked against my lower abs. It was aching. He smiled at me and took my cock in his mouth, slowly working his way up and down. He knew what he was doing— this wasn't the first cock he'd sucked, obviously. He flicked his tongue over the head, and licked my balls. I tilted my head up so I could watch him worship me.

He was almost as good at it as Blair.

My dick was wet with his spittle when he looked up and smiled at me. "Dude, I don't know if I can handle that big thing, but I sure as hell want to try."

"Let's find out then."

He put a condom on me, and squirted lube on it. He spread it all over my hard cock, and squirted more into his hand, reaching back to get his hole ready for me. He climbed back up on top of me, and moaned as he put the tip inside of him. He looked down at me. "Dude, I really don't know."

"Quit talking and do it," I said. It was odd, maybe it was the cocaine, but I wanted to feel my cock all the way inside of him. I wanted to fuck him hard, rip his asshole to shreds—ride him like no one had ever ridden his hot, tight ass before. Maybe it was because he was the pledge master and I was used to taking orders from him—but I wanted to make him submissive to me. I wanted to show him that he might be a brother, he might be older, but damn it to hell, I was a *man* and I was going to fuck him like he'd never been fucked before. I wanted to drive him crazy with pleasure. I wanted him to compare every single man who fucked him in the future and have them come up lacking. I wanted to fuck him so hard that when he saw me again his ass would tingle from the memory of my cock.

"All right," he whispered, and gasped as he slid down a little farther on my dick. His ass was very tight; I was almost afraid that if I started riding him it might rip the skin off my dick.

He was definitely going to have to get used to me before I tore into him.

"Come on, take it all," I said in a gruff voice. "Don't be a pussy, Marc. You know you want it."

He gave me a look I couldn't read, and slid down still farther—this time going all the way down. His eyes shut and he moaned, loudly—and I was grateful for REM singing on his stereo. His whole body convulsed as he sat there, more moans coming out of his throat, and then his eyes opened and he grinned. "You have no idea how incredible that fucking feels. My God, that's an awesome cock."

"Ride it buddy," I growled at him. "Make me come, brother."

"Oh, fuck yeah," he replied, and started sliding up again. When he slid down, he moaned again, his eyes closing yet again, and then his body started shaking . . . and suddenly he was spraying my chest with come.

"Oh my fucking God." He slid off of me. "I'm so sorry, man."

"It's okay."

"It just—it just felt so good I couldn't help it, man!"

I laughed and reached for a towel and wiped his come off me. I stood up and pulled my underwear and pants back up. "Thanks, Marc."

"You sure I can't finish you off?" he reached down and felt my cock through my jeans. "Damn, that sure is amazing."

"I should go wait for Blair," I said.

It was weird that I didn't care about getting off.

What I cared about was snorting some more coke.

The feeling and numbness from the first line had worn off while Marc was riding me. And I wanted that feeling back.

And suddenly, I knew that was how addiction started.

I needed to get out of that room.

Oh, man, what have I done?

I pulled on my shirt and kissed Marc on the cheek. "Thanks, man." And I escaped out the door.

I walked around the corner into the downstairs hallway just as Blair walked in the downstairs door. He was weaving a little bit. "Hey!" he grinned. "I was looking for you to see if you wanted to go with us to Denny's."

"Ah, I was wondering where you went," I said as he unlocked the door. I jumped onto the bed. "Shut the door and come over here."

"Do you mind if we don't do anything?" he asked as he undressed. "I'm really drunk, and don't feel so hot."

"No problem," I said, undressing myself. *You're not the only one*, I thought guiltily. I knew I was going to have to tell him, but it could keep until the morning, when he was sober.

When we were both naked, we got under the covers, and I held his warm body close to mine. Within a few moments, he was gently snoring.

It took me a while, but eventually, I too, fell asleep.

Chapter 8

My heart was racing as I climbed the steps to Chris and Eric's apartment.

I felt nauseous and sick to my stomach, emotionally drained and what I really wanted to do was just go hide somewhere and cry.

How could Blair be so cruel?

"Wake up," he'd said, shaking me awake the morning before.

My head hurt, my teeth felt like they'd grown hair, and my stomach was acting like an alien creature. "Morning," I'd said, sitting up in the bed.

He was pacing about the room. "I can't fucking believe you."

"What?" I asked, finally sensing that he was completely furious—at me. I shook my head a little to clear it. My heart sank. He'd found out somehow."What's the matter?"

"You fucked Marc Kearney last night, didn't you?" he snapped.

"Blair, are you serious?" I stared at him. My head ached.

"How could you do that?" he demanded. "I mean, Jesus

fucking Christ. I thought you were this sweet kid . . . and you just run around this place like a fucking dog in heat. What is with you?"

"Wait just a minute." I climbed out of the bed, and pulled my pants on. "Can you calm down for just a second?" I pulled on my Mai Tai Wun On shirt, and sat back down on the bed. "Now, I'm confused here, Blair. Really. I mean, you went to Denny's without even telling me you were leaving—let alone where. And so I needed a place to hang out because you'd locked me out of *your* room. Admitted, I shouldn't have done anything with Marc—"

"No you shouldn't have!"

"—But even still, I don't understand why you're so mad about it. What's the big deal?"

He sat down in his desk chair. "If you can't see why this is a big deal, maybe you should just leave." He shook his head. "I don't know you at all."

"What? Blair, you aren't making sense," I replied, my mood sinking more with every passing second. "Please, Blair, let's talk about this."

"Get out of my room." He spun away from me and turned on his computer. "Get out of my sight, and get out of my life."

I put on my socks and shoes. My heart sinking, I walked over to the door. I opened it and stood there for a moment. "Blair—"

He didn't answer.

I closed the door behind me.

I managed to somehow get all the way home, have a slight conversation with my parents about the party, and went to my room. I shut the door behind me and lay down on my bed before finally giving way and letting the tears come.

I really couldn't even blame the cocaine or being drunk for it. I knew when Marc and I started messing around we shouldn't be doing it. It was wrong not only to fuck my pledge master, but it was wrong because I was in love with Blair. So what if Blair didn't love me back—I loved him, and that was all that mattered. And Blair obviously cared—otherwise he wouldn't have gotten so upset. So why couldn't he just tell me sometime that he loved me? That he didn't want me being with anyone else? If Blair had ever said one word about anything like that I would have never in a million years let things with Marc get as far as they did. There was, in fact, a lot I didn't know about Blair. He didn't ever talk about his past or guys he'd been with—but I had told him all about Kevin. I'd told him about the guy in the park back in Emporia, and I'd told him about sucking Rory's dick. Blair never said anything about past loves or men, and that was odd. Maybe someone he loved hurt him. Maybe that was why he was so resistant to me saying I loved him, why he couldn't bring himself to say the words to me. We'd never talked, once, about what we meant to each other or what we were doing. We just kind of went from day to day, drifting . . . and I'd fucked that all up.

But how in the hell did Blair find out about it in the first place?

No one was around when I left Marc's room, so no one could have seen me slip out of his room.

Marc must have told him.

Oh dear God in heaven.

There was no way I could show my face around the house again.

As I lay there in my bed, I reached for my cell phone and dialed Blair's. After a few rings, it switched over to voicemail. "Blair, this is Jeff. Will you please call me back? We need to talk . . . about so many things." My voice broke. "I'm sorry about what happened last night, you may never know how sorry I really am . . . will you please call me? We have to talk about this. I can't bear the thought of you hating me . . . please." I closed my phone and tapped it to my head. I started crying again. It couldn't be over, it just couldn't.

I turned over onto my side with my phone in my hand.

If Blair doesn't call me back this weekend, on Monday morning I'm going by the house and returning my pledge pin, I decided, and fell asleep.

He didn't call. I sat there in my room waiting for my phone to ring all day Saturday. I cried myself to sleep on Saturday night. Several times I started dialing his number again but wouldn't allow myself to finish the call. No, calling him again wouldn't do any good. More messages wouldn't help, wouldn't convince him to call me. He'd call me if he damned well felt like it.

I slept late on Sunday and woke up feeling a little better. I took a shower and brushed my teeth. Mom and Dad were at church, so I had a bowl of Cheerios and some coffee. I tried to put Blair out of my head, but my mind kept drifting back to him. And at some point, the hurt started turning to anger.

Fuck him. He could have the decency to call me back. Yes, I was wrong for sleeping with Marc, but for all I know he could be fucking half the house. I'm not there 24/7—and if he cared about me at all he would have called by now. Fuck him, and fuck Beta Kappa. If he hasn't called me by the time I go to bed tonight I am dropping off my pledge pin to Marc tomorrow and I am done with the whole thing. Might as well get caught up on my studying. And maybe, just maybe, if he ever does bother to call, it might just be too late.

I was pretty behind on my studying. Between spending every available moment I had at the house, I hadn't cracked a book all semester. And as I went through my course outlines, I realized with horror that I had a test coming up over the next two weeks in every class—and a couple of papers to write.

I was working my way through my English Comp reading when my phone rang, making me jump. I grabbed it without looking at the caller ID, hoping it was Blair. "Hello?"

"Dude, what you up to?" It was Chris Moore.

"Nothing, studying. Man, I am so fucking behind."

"Yeah I know what you mean. I have an Econ test Wednesday and I haven't even opened the book. Probably stay up all night Tuesday and study. How you doing?"

"Okay, I guess. Why?"

"Yeah, well people were wondering where you were yesterday for the clean-up day."

"Oh, shit, I completely forgot." The brotherhood had declared a mandatory pledge clean up day for Saturday, to return the house to normal after the big luau party. I was so wrapped up in Blair being mad at me I'd completely forgotten. *Ah, just as well, since I'm depledging tomorrow, who cares if the brothers are pissed at me or I look bad*, I thought.

"Don't worry, we covered for you." Chris laughed. "Told Marc you had a major test on Monday and had to spend the weekend studying. *Alma mater first*, and all that bullshit, right?"

"Right." I wanted to ask if Blair had asked about me, had said anything, but kept my mouth shut. "Thanks, man."

"Well, Eric and I were wondering if you wanted to come over for a little bit," he said quietly, "you know, just to hang out and stuff? I mean, if you aren't doing anything else. But if you really have to study . . ." his voice trailed off.

I flashed back to just before the party, when he and I had sat on Blair's bed getting stoned. *It was so hot watching you and Eric wrestle . . . you should come over sometime and . . .* I remembered him putting his hand on my dick. He and Eric were sexy. And Blair could just go to hell. I didn't owe him anything. But I did need to study. I opened my mouth to say "No thank you, some other time," but then I saw the clock. It was almost seven P.M. on Sunday night. I had called him when I got home around ten on Saturday morning— and he still hadn't called me back.

You don't owe him a goddamned thing. Fuck him. He yells at you, throws you out of his room for breaking some rule you didn't even know existed, and then doesn't have the decency to call you back? Why not have some fun?

"Sure, great," I said, closing my textbook, and slipping it into my backpack. "I'm on my way."

"Cool, see you in a few!" Chris hung up.

Chris and Eric's apartment was in the Valencia Apartments complex, which sounded a lot nicer than it actually was. On the street that ran along the back of the university campus and the stadium, across from the stadium were the two story buildings that made up the Valencia. I'm sure when they were first built; back after the second World War they were probably really decent and affordable apartments for the CSUP students who lived there. But year after year of college students, parties, and destruction had taken their toll on the Valencia, and now they were just kind of tired and sad. The stucco facades had cracks in them, and the paint on the walls inside looked like the original paint. The carpets had cigarette burns in them and years of spills soaked up. Chris and Eric often joked about naming the roaches in their kitchen and training them as pets. We always had our pledge meetings there because their apartment was so close to the house, and also because Chris was the president of our class.

As I drove the Flying Couch on the familiar way I always took to see Blair at the house, I felt a sob welling up in my throat. Surely it couldn't end this way between us? It wasn't right, especially over something as stupid as me sleeping with Marc Kearney—a stupid mistake that would never in a million years happen again. How could I have been so stupid?

I fought to get control of myself. I didn't want Chris and Eric to see me like this, and after all, what had I done that was so wrong?

This time, though, I couldn't convince myself.

By the time I knocked on Chris and Eric's door, I was worked up into an incredibly high emotional state again. When Eric opened the door, he did a double take. "Dude, are you okay? You look awful."

"Nice to see you, too." I pushed past him into their living room. All the furniture had been pushed up against the walls and there were two mattresses pushed together in the center of the floor. Chris was sitting at their dining table, rolling joints with an open bottle of beer to one side of the tray where he was sorting seeds and stems out from the marijuana chaff.

"Grab a beer," Chris instructed without looking up from the joint he was rolling. I grabbed one and removed the top before sitting down at the table. Chris looked up and grinned at me. "Glad you could make it, man." He picked up a joint and put one end into his mouth, lighting the other side. He passed me the joint and I took a hit.

Eric came up from behind me, and leaned down, running his hands up and down my torso. "Wrestling you on Big Brother Night was so hot—well, what I remember of it anyway," he said, taking the joint from me. "It's a good thing I was so drunk otherwise I'd have popped a big ol' boner. Damn, man, you have a fine ass."

The pot started relaxing me, and I giggled. "Yeah, well, you're pretty hot yourself there, buddy. I was afraid I would, too—but with so many people around and watching, I guess I was shy."

Eric kissed my neck, and I could feel my dick starting to come to life. "Well, stud, we can go for it tonight. Got the mattresses all set up. And you're not winning this time, now that I'm actually sober."

"Oh, you think?" I teased, winking at Chris.

"He's all talk, you know." Chris laughed, taking the joint away from Eric and taking a hit. "I kick his ass on a regular basis. He likes having his ass kicked." He winked back at me. "It turns him on, you know. He likes being dominated." He rolled his eyes. "You should hear him squeal when he has a dick up his ass."

I laughed. The pot was definitely helping, and I loved these two.

"Fuck you," Eric said easily, without malice. "You know I let you win because it makes you so hot." He nibbled on my earlobe, which made me moan a little bit. I turned my head into his mouth. "It fucking drives him crazy to win . . . keep that in mind when we get down to it, okay?"

"Okay, I think I've got it. Chris likes to win, and you like to lose. Easy enough." I laughed and took a sip of my beer. "How long have you two been—" I hesitated. I wasn't really sure how to put it. At parties—especially during Little Sister Rush, the two of them were the biggest horn dogs in the pledge class, going after anything with tits that moved.

Chris reached over and took my hand. "Eric and I have been messing around since we were about twelve, I think. We're bisexual—we like girls too. But guys"—he laughed— "guys are a lot of fun, too. Of course, we have each other so we can always get laid whenever either one of us is horny—"

"Which pretty much is all the time," Eric went on, sliding his big hands down over my crotch, "so if we don't feel like messing with chicks or anything, we just take care of each other."

"It's not like we're in love or anything," Chris explained. "I mean, we're best friends, sure, but we're not in love with each other. It's just a physical thing for us."

"Wow." I took another hit. I was feeling quite pleasant. It was very good pot, and Eric's hand rubbing on my dick was having a predictable effect. I didn't understand their arrangement completely, but it made perfect sense the way they described it. Maybe that was the problem with Blair and I—I certainly had crossed the line from friendship into love, and the way he reacted—he had to have as well. "Have you messed around with anyone in the house?"

They looked at each other and started laughing. "I sucked Rory Armagh off," Eric said after a moment. "Jesus. He sure has a horsedick."

"I did too!" I laughed. "I don't know how I got that huge thing down my throat."

"You were able to?" Eric moved around and sat down, giving me an admiring glance. "I couldn't, I just did as much as I could until he shot his wad. I mean, when I saw that thing it scared the crap out of me. He's deformed."

"I fucked Marc Kearney," Chris offered. "Pledge master my ass. Big ol' insatiable bottom is what he is."

"You've fucked Blair, haven't you?" Eric asked. "You might as well tell the truth—we've thought so almost from the start of the semester."

"It's the way he looks at you," Chris chimed in. "I mean, when you don't know he's looking at you? He's in love with you, if you haven't done anything with him."

"Yeah," I said in a small voice. "Blair and I have been together. Since last summer. But not anymore." I bit my lip. "I did something stupid the other night and now he hates me."

"He'll get over it," Eric said with a lot more confidence than I certainly felt. "Seriously, Jeff, I'm not making this shit up. He might be mad now, but he does love you. Just give it some time, trust me on this, okay?"

"What did you do?" Chris asked.

"It embarrassed me to admit it, but Friday night I was supposed to spend the night in his room, but when the party was over I couldn't find him—"

"He went to Denny's. We were there," Eric broke in. "We wondered where you were. You two are almost always together."

"Well, when I was looking for him I wound up in Marc's room."

Chris let out a loud laugh. "And you fucked Marc, Marc told Blair, and now he's pissed at you."

"Yeah, that's pretty much it," I said, looking down at my hands.

"So Blair doesn't like you to mess around with other guys?" Chris asked. "Then maybe we shouldn't—"

"Fuck him, he doesn't own me," I said with more bravado than I actually felt.

"Okay, then." Eric grinned. "You guys ready to wrestle?"

I made eye contact with Chris, who just rolled his eyes, which made me laugh. "Okay, let's kick some Matthews ass, shall we?"

Chris stripped off his sweatshirt as he walked into the living room, and pulled off his sweatpants as well. He stood there stark naked, and smiled. His body was amazing. He was tanned except for a square area of white just below his navel that ran to his upper thighs. His cock was long, hard and thick, and his balls were round and heavy. "Come on, Jeff, don't be shy." He took his cock in one hand. "Don't let this intimidate you. Not everyone can be as hung as I am."

"Fuck you. That little thing ain't nothing," I replied as Eric dropped his shorts and tossed them on the couch. Now, he too was naked. His cock stood out straight away from his body, and I saw with a bit of surprise he was uncircumcised. His dick wasn't as long as Chris's, but it had a slight bend in it and was somewhat thicker. He and Chris stepped up on to the mattresses and started circling each other as I pulled off my shirt. I took off my sandals, and after a moment's hesitation, slid my shorts and underwear down, folding them in half and placing them on the table. I walked into the living room just as Chris took Eric down to the mattresses, slid on to his back and locked a full nelson on him. The muscles in Chris's back strained as he applied pressure, rubbing his dick on Eric's ass. "Say it, big guy, you know you want to," Chris said.

"Fuck you!" Eric replied, trying to power his arms down to break the hold.

My dick was hard as granite. I sat down on the couch to

watch. Chris looked over at me and winked. "See, I told you he likes to get dominated. It turns him on." Then he did a double take. "Damn, you are big, buddy!"

"Fuck you!" Eric said again.

"You want some of this, Jeff?" Chris grinned. "It's nice having this hot ass under your dick. Trust me, you'll like it!" He started thrusting his hips, rubbing his cock inside Eric's ass crack. "Yeah, bitch, you want that big cock inside you, don't you?"

"Fuck you BOTH!" Eric gasped out.

With a grin of my own, I stood up and walked over to them. I knelt down in front of Eric's face, then grabbed a handful of hair and pulled his head up. "I don't think you're in any position to be so snotty, Eric."

"Slap his face—just not real hard," Chris instructed.

Gently I slapped his face. He moaned. I looked up at Chris, who nodded. I slapped him again, a little harder this time. "You asshole," he gasped out.

"Asshole?" I smacked his face again.

"When I get out of this I am going to kick both your asses!"

With a laugh, Chris let go of him and stood up. Playfully he reached down and smacked Eric's ass. "Well?"

I climbed up on the mattress. This was fun. "Come on then, you big pussy! I kicked your ass once before! Can't wait to do it again!"

Eric and I started circling each other, while Chris went into the other room to get a joint. Eric lunged for my legs, and I let them slide out behind me, putting all my weight on his back. We both dropped down to the mattress, with me on top of him. "Damn it," he grunted underneath me. I managed to spin around on his back so I was behind him, and slid my arms under his armpits, slapping the same full nelson on him Chris had used.

Chris was right. His ass did feel nice under my cock. I started rubbing my cock on his hard ass.

Chris started laughing. "Eric, you just suck. You could at least try!"

"Fuck you both!"

Eric was trying to free himself from the nelson, and it was taking everything I had to keep him trapped. *Damn, he's strong,* I thought, *if I ever let him catch me I'm getting my ass kicked for sure.*

Chris walked over and knelt down in front of Eric. "You know, the only thing hotter than kicking your ass is watching someone else do it."

"Fuck you both!"

"The only person around here who's getting fucked, my friend, is you." Chris winked at me. He pulled Eric's head up and slapped him in the face with his cock. "How's that, big man? You like having my cock rubbed all over your face?"

Eric stopped struggling underneath me. Instead, he arched his lower back and ground his ass into my cock. "Mmm, let me suck that big thing, please."

"I don't know." Chris looked at me. "What do you think, Jeff? Should we let this pig suck on my cock?"

I repressed a grin and replied in an equally serious tone, "Well, I don't know. Does the pig want my big cock up his ass?"

Eric was silent for a moment. "Oh, hell yes I do, big man!" he roared in answer, grinding his ass up at me again.

Damn, I wanted to fuck him. I burned with desire for his big body.

"Then what are you waiting for?" Chris laughed. "Let him up, Jeff."

I let him go, and got off his back. Eric got up on all fours, arching his back so that his muscular ass was up in the air with the cheeks spread wide apart, Chris got up to his knees, and Eric took him into his mouth. I put on a condom, lubed up my dick, and took aim. *Be ready, Eric*, I thought, *you're getting it all on the first thrust.*

I took a deep breath and shoved my cock all the way inside of him. Once I was inside all the way, I stayed there, and started moving my hips around in a circular motion. Eric stopped sucking Chris's cock, and looked back over his shoulder. "Fuck yeah, Jeff, fuck me man, fuck me, give it all to me, man."

Chris slapped Eric's face with his cock. "What did I tell you, man? He's a fucking pig."

I started moving back and forth, pulling out slow, then slamming into him as fast and hard as I could. Eric kept up the patter, and when I looked over at Chris, he was stroking his own dick.

"Yeah, that's hot," he said when our eyes met. "Fuck him, and fuck him hard, man."

I looked Chris's body over. He was so damned muscular and sexy—so was Eric, for that matter. I kept pounding away, working in a rhythm. With every penetration Eric would let out a loud gasp, and then would go back to talking nasty.

"Yeah, give me that big cock, man, fuck me hard, rip me in half, man, that's the way I like it, come on, yeah fuck me man, fuck me . . ."

It was so sexy, such a turn-on, that it didn't take long for me to start to shoot my load.

I pulled my cock out of his ass just as Chris shot a big load all over Eric's back.

"Oh, man." Eric rolled over onto his stomach. "Man, that was so fucking hot. Any time you want to fuck me, you just let me know." He sat up, "Chris, I fucking came without touching myself."

I got to my feet, peeling the condom off. I carried it into the kitchen and dumped it in the trash. I walked back into the living room. Chris and Eric were lying on the mattresses, their arms around each other, kissing. I stood there for a moment, watching them.

I miss Blair, I thought, and choked down a sob.

I picked up my clothes and started getting dressed.

"Hey, don't go," Eric said drowsily. "Come cuddle with us."

"I can't," I said. "I appreciate it, but I really need to get going."

"Anytime, man," Chris said. "Anytime at all you wanna come back over, we're here for ya, man. And everything's going to be fine with Blair, you just wait and see. He loves you, man."

I walked over and kissed him lightly on the mouth, then kissed Eric too. "Thanks. You guys are the best." I walked out of the apartment and took a deep breath. *You might as well get used to not having Blair anymore. And Chris and Eric are fun. Who knows where it all might lead? So they aren't Blair. Get over it.*

My phone rang when I got to my car. I looked at the caller ID. "Blair?" I answered it, my heart starting to race.

"I'm sorry I was such a dickhead. I miss you. Can you come over?"

"I'll be there in five minutes."

"I love you."

I sat there, not believing my ears. "What did you say?"

"I love you." He said it again, more quietly this time. "I love you and I want you to be with me. Always. Can you forgive me for being such an asshole?" His voice broke. "I don't care if you fuck everyone in the house, as long as I'm the one you care the most about."

"Oh, Blair." I started to cry. "I love you so much. I'll be right there."

I started my car and headed over to the house.

Chapter 9

Sensory deprivation has to be the worst torture ever thought up by a human being.

Blindfolded, with a rag tied around my hand, I sat on the floor in what I thought just might be the Great Room, but couldn't be sure. The floor was hard under my ass, and all I could hear was this horrible noise that sounded like a cross between whale songs and shattering glass. It was loud, so incredibly loud I couldn't hear anything else.

I was also incredibly tired. It was the Thursday night of what the brothers euphemistically called "Inspiration Week" in a nod to the university's (and the national chapter's) stance on hazing—but it really *was* Hell Week.

The week started with us arriving on Sunday night and lining up under the basketball hoop. We stood out there in our dress clothes, holding paper bags from the grocery store with the supplies they told us to bring: a toothbrush and toothpaste, a brick, a T-shirt, a pair of jeans, a pair of white socks, a black magic marker, a pack of chewing gum, and our black books. We also had a bag with clothes for the week. We stood out there silently, all twelve of us—somehow Ted had managed to make it through the whole semester, no matter how much we wanted him to quit—waiting until, at six P.M. on the dot, Marc Kearney came solemnly walking out of the house to us.

"I keep waiting for that music from *The Good the Bad and the Ugly* to start playing," Chris whispered to me out of the side of his mouth, and I suppressed a laugh.

"Will you two shut up? You're going to get us all in trouble," Ted hissed from my other side.

We just looked at each other and rolled our eyes.

I don't know really what I was expecting out of Hell Week, but the reality was nothing I could have imagined. Marc led us into the house single file, and like on Big Brother Night, we lined up against the wall in the Great Room.

The brotherhood stood in a crowd facing us. I swallowed. Marc stepped out in front of the crowd, holding a clipboard, a whistle around his neck.

"Welcome to Hell Week, pledges," he said, smiling as he walked up and down in front of us. As he passed me, I shifted from one foot to the other. Ever since the night I'd fucked him, he'd been noticeably cool to me. Sometimes I thought I was just being paranoid, and others I thought I was right. I tried to find Blair's face in the crowd, but couldn't. I had a sinking feeling in the pit of my stomach. *This is not going to be good*, kept running through my head. "Will your big brothers please step forward and stand in front of your pledge?" I felt some relief when Blair stepped in front of me, his face was solemn, but he winked at me. "Please remove your little brother's pledge pin." Blair reached up and removed mine. "Pledges, you no longer will be required to wear your pledge pin in public. It is now a thing of the past. However," he paused, "you will be replacing your pledge pin with the brick you were told to bring with you. You will carry it with you everywhere—as long as you are on Beta Kappa property. When you are at class or at work you will leave it with your other belongings in the chapter room—it will be safe as long as you are off property. However, when you return to property, you must have it on you at all times—or your entire pledge class will suffer the consequences."

He continued with the rules of the week, and my heart sank with each new one. We were not allowed to eat or drink or sleep until we were released on Thursday morning. As long as we were on property, we had to wear the jeans and white T-shirt. Whenever the whistle blew, no matter where we were in the house, we had to run down to the Great Room and line up in alphabetical order on the wall. While we were on property—unless we were studying for a test—we were at the disposal of the brotherhood; anyone could make us do anything they wanted us to. We would be cleaning the house in preparation for the Initiation Ritual on Friday night—provided we made it through the week. At any time during the week, any one of us could be bounced from the program at any moment by a vote by the brotherhood. We were a unit; and the transgressions of one were visited upon the whole. And when the whistle blew, we not only had to lineup on the wall, we had to hold it up—which meant flattening our back against it, bending our legs at the knee until they were at a ninety degree angle, and holding our pledge brick out in front of us with both hands until we were told to stand up.

"Now, put all of your things in the chapter room, and put on your pledge uniform," Marc went on. "That will be your home until you are released Thursday morning; unless of course you are dismissed any time before then. You need to take your magic markers, and on the front of your T-shirts you are to write Beta Kappa Pledge Class, Fall 2006. On your bricks, on one side you will write Beta Kappa, on another your pledge class. And when you hear the whistle, you need to get to the wall as quickly as possible and hold the position."

And so it began, four nights of mental and physical abuse. I learned to loathe the sound of the whistle; I was certain the sound of it would haunt my dreams for the rest of my life. Brothers I'd considered to be benign and friendly turned vicious and sadomasochistic, screaming in my face for not being properly deferential or some other imagined transgression. We were forced to do push-ups and hold that damned wall until our legs ached. I cleaned urinals with a toothbrush, gagging over the foul smell of sour urine. I would finish one only to have a brother come in and use it, and then scream at me to clean the one he'd just used. What I really wanted to do was knock him down and shove the filthy toothbrush in his mouth, but instead I simply shouted "SIR! YES SIR!" back at him and went to work. And finally, at around three in the morning, they finally dismissed us and let us go into the chapter room to sleep for a few hours—they would be waking us at six in the morning.

When we were on campus, we were supposed to avoid the brothers—and if it couldn't be helped, we weren't allowed to make eye contact. After I finished my last class at noon that Monday, I was starving. I'd managed to get some drinks of water out of fountains on campus when I was certain no brother was anywhere around. As I trudged back to the house, a car pulled up to the curb. Inside were three brothers, including Rory Armagh. "Hey, Jeff, get in the car." Rory opened the back door. A bit hesitantly, I climbed in, and once I'd shut the door they drove off and headed for the Carl's Jr. about five blocks away from the house. "What do you want to eat?" Rory asked as we idled in the drive through.

"Nothing," I replied.

David Jensen, a senior who was driving the car, started laughing. "This isn't a trap, Jeff. Nobody really expects you to starve yourself till Thursday morning. Didn't your big brother tell you? Brothers and little sisters will feed you— you just can't get caught or turned in by anyone. And we're not going to turn you in."

I took a deep breath. "Western bacon cheeseburger, large order of fries, and large Coke." My stomach growled at the thought of food. Once we got our order, they pulled over into a parking spot and I scarfed it all down in record time. Rory patted me on the leg as they drove back to the house, letting me out exactly where they picked me up. "It's all a game, Jeff," Rory whispered before I got out of the car, "just remember that. And before you know it, it's all over and you're a brother."

I got out of the car and stood there for a moment, watching them as they drove off. *Why didn't Blair explain any of this to me?* I wondered. Ever since the incident with Marc Kearney, we'd seemed so much closer. Every time we were together, Blair would tell me how much he loved me. So why didn't he explain to me how I was going to survive Hell Week? *Maybe he's punishing you for fucking Marc Kearney.*

I didn't like that thought.

But knowing I was going to get fed and given something to drink from time to time made the asshole behavior of the brothers while I was in the house somewhat easier to take. The irony was that I actually wound up eating more during Hell Week than I would have if I'd been eating normally. You could never tell a brother or a little sister that you weren't hungry—stupid ass Ted made that mistake, and the brother got him to admit he'd been fed by a little sister half an hour earlier, and the brother ratted him out. That cost us all five minutes holding the wall and one hundred push-ups.

Needless to say, this didn't increase Ted's popularity with his pledge brothers.

Monday night we were taught a lesson.

At one in the morning, we were sent to the chapter room and told to strip naked to wait for the whistle. "What do you suppose they are going to do to us?" Ted asked in a whimper.

"Maybe we're going to all take it up the ass," Eric said nastily, and a couple of the rest of us laughed.

"You'd like that, wouldn't you?" Ted shot back.

Eric's face turned red, and there was no telling what would have happened next. Fortunately, there was a knock on the chapter room door, and then Marc opened it. "No laughter in the chapter room," he said severely. "When you're in here, you should be quiet and thinking about what you can bring to the Brotherhood *if* you get initiated."

We all looked down.

"Pledge Amundsen, come with me."

Tommy Amundsen, the sophomore from Mission Viejo, who'd once told me his ambition was to one day be White House Chief of Staff, looked like nothing more than a terrified country mouse going to his doom. We sat there in silence, straining to hear what was going on out in the Great

Room. We couldn't hear a thing, other than Marc knocking on the door before sticking his head in and taking the next pledge in alphabetical order.

When it was my turn, I swallowed and stood up. I made my face neutral, void of expression, and held my head high as I walked out there behind Marc. The brothers were standing in a circle, each holding a candle. Marc led me to the center of the circle. "Brotherhood of Beta Kappa, I present to you Jeffrey Morgan, a candidate to join your circle." He intoned, and then took a candle and joined the circle.

"Candidate Morgan, why do you seek to join the Brotherhood?" someone whose voice I couldn't recognize asked from behind me.

I cleared my throat. "Because I believe in what the Brotherhood stands for."

There were murmured sounds of approval.

"Candidate Morgan, what do you have to offer to the Brotherhood?" This question was unmistakably from Jerry Pollard, who was directly in front of me.

"My lifelong devotion and commitment to the preservation of the Brotherhood's ideals," I replied, trying to keep my voice from shaking. *World peace* flashed through my mind and I struggled to repress a nervous giggle. Somehow, standing naked in front of the brothers, I didn't think laughing was appropriate.

"Candidate Morgan, what would you be willing to do to prove to the Brotherhood that you want to become a part of us?" There was no mistaking that voice. It was Blair.

"Anything, sir." I raised my chin defiantly.

Again, murmurs of approval.

"All right, Prospective Brother Morgan, please follow me," Marc said, and led me to the kitchen where my fellow pledges were all standing. "And be quiet in here!" Marc said, before closing the door behind him.

"Man, I had no idea what to say in there," Chris whispered to me. "But you did okay, I made an ass out of myself."

"Well," Eric said on the other side of me, "no matter how bad any of us might blow it, no one will blow it quite as bad as Ted is going to."

Sure enough, it wasn't long before we heard the Brotherhood hooting and hissing. The group of us in the kitchen let out a collective groan. "Maybe they'll throw him out," Eric said hopefully.

"We should be so lucky," Tommy Amundsen said venomously.

A few moments later, the kitchen door opened and a redfaced Ted came in. Marc's face was thunderous. "Maybe," he spat out, "you should talk to your pledge brothers about what Beta Kappa means to them, maggot, and maybe later we'll give you another chance."

The door slammed shut behind him.

"What the fuck did you say?" Chris hissed, grabbing Ted by the arm.

"Let go of me!" Ted whined, pulling his arm away. "I answered them honestly, like we were supposed to." He stepped away from us. "I didn't suck up to them the way you all did, obviously."

I took a breath and counted to three. In that moment, all I wanted to do was smack him across the face. I've never hated anyone in my life as much as I hated Ted Norris in that moment. I would have cheerfully strangled him to death right then and there, and my pledge brothers would have cheered me on.

Instead, we all just shook our heads and looked away from him.

After Rob Ross, our final pledge brother, was led in, the Brotherhood left us in the kitchen for what seemed like hours. We could hear them talking out there, and occasionally there would be a chorus of finger snaps. The clock on the wall read one-fifteen when Marc finally came back into the kitchen.

"Prospectives, eleven of you answered the Brotherhood's questions to our satisfaction," he said in that solemn voice he'd been using to address us since Sunday night. "However, one of you did not. As I explained to you on the first night of your journey, you are a unit. If one of you fails, all of you fail. Therefore, the Brotherhood has collectively decided as one that your class has failed your test this evening." He held up his hand for silence as all of us began talking, swearing, or muttering. "However, rather than depledging your entire class and having you start over next semester, the Brotherhood has decided that if one of you agrees to take punishment for the entire class' failure, this will be an appropriate show of unity, and you may all continue."

"Do it, Ted," Chris snarled.

Ted just stood there for a moment, looking down at the ground. He didn't say anything.

"Only one of you is required," Marc said after a few moments.

"I'll do it." I stepped forward. "I will take the punishment for the entire class, Brother Kearney."

"You are certain?"

"Yes, sir."

He nodded. "The rest of your pledge brothers will return

to the chapter room and dress. We will come for you when we are ready for you."

He held the door open as they filed out. Ted was the only one who wouldn't meet my eyes—everyone else touched me on the shoulder or arm to thank me.

To be honest, I was absolutely terrified. I had no idea what was going to happen, what kind of punishment I was about to take—but one thing was for sure, if it took the rest of my life, Ted Norris would pay for it somehow. After they had all gone, Marc came over to me. "I'll be back in a little while for you. Are you sure you want to do this, Jeff?" he said in his normal voice.

I raised my chin. "Yes, sir."

"I'm sorry, Jeff." He put his arms around me and squeezed me. "I know I wasn't really friendly to you after, well, you know"—he hesitated—"but Blair was so mad about it,I didn't really want to give him any reason to think, well, you know." He swallowed. "But you're a great guy. Jeff. I wish you were my little brother instead of Blair's. You really understand what Beta Kappa is all about. I respect you, man." He shook his head. "I can't tell you how disappointed I am in Ted. I really expected him to step up to the plate after he screwed up. He is so not a true Beta Kappa, but now it's too late to do anything about it. How many chances do you have to give someone, you know?"

"I'm sorry, too, Marc." I replied, my heart swelling with pride. *My pledge master thinks I am a true Beta Kappa!* And at the same time, I felt sorry for Ted. I couldn't imagine how awful it would be to have the pledge master disappointed in you. I couldn't understand why he even wanted to be in the Brotherhood. He didn't seem to understand the con-

cept of brotherhood, of selflessness, of being a part of something that was greater than the sum of its parts.

"Good luck, Jeff." He hugged me again and brushed his
lips against my cheek. "I'll be back in a little bit for you."

Afterwards, when my pledge brothers asked me about it,
I told them honestly that the waiting was the worst part of
it. As I stood there, naked, in the darkened kitchen, my
mind raced through a million possibilities of what my punishment would be. There was realistically no telling what it
could be. All I could hope for was something benign. But
then again, there were all those paddles hanging on the
walls of the Great Room—and no matter how many times
the brothers told me they were symbolic of the hazing days
of the past and had no real modern day significance, I always wondered. I tried to focus on remaining calm, master-
ing my mind and not letting it think dark thoughts like that.
This was a sacrifice I was making for my pledge brothers, so
we wouldn't have to start over again in the spring semester,
and that was the most important thing. I cleared my mind
of my anger and animosity toward Ted.

And when Marc came back for me, I was ready.

When he led me back into the Great Room, it was impossible not to notice the big round wooden object mounted
on the wall where we always lined up. There were four
straps, two up high and two down low. I inhaled sharply.
"Pledge Morgan, are you ready to take the punishment on
behalf of your entire pledge class?"

"SIR! YES SIR!" I shouted as loudly as I could, even
though I felt like I was going to faint at any moment.

"Please approach the Wheel." Marc said.

I started walking over to it, and the Brotherhood parted
to let me through. It was also impossible not to notice that

every paddle had been removed from the walls, and every brother I passed was holding one. *I am going to be beaten, oh my God.* When I reached the Wheel, I stopped. "Step up to the Wheel," Marc ordered. I walked right up to it. "Raise your arms." I did, and two brothers stepped up, strapping my wrists to it while two other brothers strapped my ankles to it. I was completely spread-eagled. My entire body was pressed up against the cool, polished wooden surface. "Bring out the prospective brother candidates!" Marc shouted, and I heard the door to the chapter room being opened. "Candidates, step to the front!" Marc shouted. "Behold your brother, Jeffrey Morgan, who is about to take the punishment decided upon by the Brotherhood for your collective failure! Behold the justice of the Brotherhood!" In a lower voice, he went on, "His big brother will strike the first blow. Step forward, Brother Blanchard. Strike whenever you are ready."

I was conscious of someone behind me, and my entire body tensed. Blair leaned forward and whispered in my ear, "Relax, Jeff. If you're tense it will hurt more. Trust me. Let your ass go limp."

"Okay." I managed to gasp out. My heart was racing.

The Brotherhood began to hum, a low sound that built until just as Blair touched my ass lightly with the paddle—at which point they all shouted "WHAP!"

Blair whispered, "Most of the brothers will not hit you any harder than that. But some will—some are sadistic assholes when it comes to this kind of thing."

And so it began. Blair was right—the next three people who swung at my ass just lightly touched it. But whoever the next brother was, put everything he had into it. My entire body went rigid from the shock and the pain, and I couldn't help it, I cried out, and my eyes started watering. I didn't think I was going to be able to catch my breath, but as I struggled the next brother swung, even harder than the one before. My brain could not comprehend the excruciating pain, and my knees buckled, and I hung there from my wrists, and pain tore through my shoulders. Through the blinding agony I could hear the Brotherhood murmuring, and the next few hits were very mild. But that was how it went; a few minor taps followed by full-strength swings. Tears streamed down my face, but I refused to cry out again. I refused to allow my knees to buckle. I tried to channel the pain into anger—anger at the assholes who were hitting me so hard, anger at Ted who was the cause of this torture—and after a few more brutal blows the stinging in my ass seemed to fade as it went numb. I somehow crossed a border from intense pain to pleasure, and I began to look forward to the next blow. I don't know how it happened. It was as though the pain synapse in my brain overloaded and blew out, and the pleasure synapse opened up in its place. My cock grew hard, and I began to look forward to the next major blow. I couldn't keep quiet, I began moaning when I was struck—but it wasn't moans of pain. It was pleasure, pure pleasure, and my cock throbbed, my balls swelling with every stroke. I gave myself in to the feeling, not knowing what it meant, and the next thing I knew it was over.

And oddly, I wanted it to go on.

A soft robe was wrapped around me, and then someone was undoing the straps. When my arms came free, they were completely numb and I almost fell. In the distance, I heard Marc shout at the pledges to return to the chapter room, and as I collapsed, someone caught me and picked me up in his arms. I opened my eyes and saw Rory Armagh's face, and his eyes were filled with tears.

A million miles away I heard Blair say, "Take him to my room."

I was vaguely aware of being carried through the darkened hallway, and then gently set down on Blair's bed. As soon as my ass touched the mattress, I cried out, and Rory rolled me over onto my stomach. "Here, take this," someone said, and a pill was pressed into my mouth, and a bottle of water held up to my lips. I swallowed the pill with a big gulp of water.

"Look at his ass!" Blair said, his voice shaking with rage as he pulled the robe off me. "He isn't going to be able to sit down for a week! This is such bullshit!"

"Look, Blair, I agree with you." I recognized Marc's voice through the fog. "I can't believe people actually swung so hard—"

"They should be drummed out of the Brotherhood," Blair went on. "We should probably take him to the emergency room!"

"And then what? Lose our charter when the dean finds out?" Marc said.

Whatever pill they'd given me was starting to take effect. The throbbing was fading away, and my head felt like it was free from my body and I was floating above it all. I opened my eyes and saw Blair, Marc, and Rory. *The three brothers I've had sex with*, I thought and started giggling. Marc and Blair were still arguing somewhat, but when they heard me giggling, they stopped and stared at me.

"It's the Vicodin," Rory explained. "Must be hitting him now."

"I don't care what anyone says," Blair went on, reaching

down and stroking my head. "He's not sleeping in the chapter room tonight, and he's not answering the whistle tomorrow morning."

"I'll have to talk to the Executive Council—"

"Tell them it's an important lesson to the pledge class," Rory interrupted Marc, kneeling down and patting my forehead with a wet cold cloth. "Don't tell the pledges anything about him. Let them wonder all night and all tomorrow morning. Not a word about him to any of them."

"That's good, Rory." A smile spread over Marc's face. "They'll be terrified, and maybe Ted will learn something from this whole thing."

"And if they don't go for it," Blair replied, "you can tell them I'm calling an ambulance, and my next call will be to the fucking police."

And I fell asleep.

I stayed in Blair's room until the middle of the next afternoon, and unlike my pledge brothers, I was treated royally by the Brotherhood. Several brothers came in with food and sodas, looked at my ass, and apologized for hitting me so hard. (I later found out that the brothers who had taken real swings were placed on a two-semester probation by the Executive Council—another infraction and they would be tossed out without trial by the Brotherhood. Also, this incident almost split the house in half; the Brotherhood had met and argued for hours while I slept.) My ass was sore, and Marc came in to tell me that the Executive Council had decided to excuse me from holding the wall until Hell Week was officially over. "No," I said, "I won't be held apart from my pledge brothers. I will do whatever they do."

I returned to the chapter room around three o'clock that afternoon. I could walk—a little slowly, and sitting down was difficult, but Rory had given me the rest of his Vicadin prescription, all the little pills broken in half. "Just take a half," he'd whispered when slipping me the bottle, "if you need to. Half will dull the pain but won't fuck you up so bad that it's noticeable."

When I walked in, only one of my pledge brothers was there, of all people, it was Ted Norris. He looked up when I opened the door, and just as quickly looked away. "Hey, Ted," I said, wincing as I slid down by my stuff. "How you doing?"

When he didn't answer, I looked over at him and saw that his lower lip was trembling. "Ted, are you okay?"

"No, I'm not," he replied in a shaky voice. He still wouldn't look at me. "I don't even know why I'm still here. Everyone hates me!" He spat the words out, and then he did actually start to cry.

"No, they don't," I lied, and hated myself for lying to him.

He wiped at his eyes. "Yeah, they do, but thanks for lying. I know I don't deserve it." He looked at me, his eyes filling again. "I'm sorry about last night, Jeff, really I am. I didn't know they were going to do—that to you."

"Ted—"

"Oh, I know you all hate me. Everyone does. Everyone always does. I try so hard, you know, to make friends but nothing ever works. You all hated me almost from the start." He kept sobbing. "I wanted to belong somewhere. I wanted to have friends. I didn't want it to be the same as it's always been. But I should know better. No one ever likes me. My own big brother can't stand to be around me." He laughed bitterly. "But why am I telling you? You don't care. It's always easy for people like you and Chris and Eric, everyone always likes you. And if you didn't hate me be-

fore, you do after last night. I'm a loser. A total loser." He
buried his face in his arm.

I didn't know what to say. I felt like a complete asshole. I
couldn't imagine what it would be like to be Ted. He was
right, it has always been relatively easy for me to make
friends. And my big brother? My big brother was in love
with me.

As my pledge brothers began showing up after class, they
all gathered around me and asked me how I was doing, how
I felt, and I couldn't help but notice the dark looks they
gave Ted. Ted had pulled himself together, and his face was
an expressionless mask, reading his Biology textbook.

But when all twelve of us were in the chapter room, waiting for the six o'clock whistle, I announced, "Can I have
everyone's attention please?"

Ten faces turned to me—everyone's except Ted's.

I cleared my throat. "I have something I want to say." I
swallowed. "The first thing the Brotherhood said to us on
Sunday night was that we are one unit. They have told us
that all semester, over and over again. The reason they have
said that to us so many times is because the Brotherhood itself is a unit; a greater whole than its parts. One of the tests
they have set for us this semester was to see if we could pull
together as a unit—to see if we would be able to become a
part of the bigger unit that is the Brotherhood. And much as
I hate to say this, we have failed that test, over and over
again."

"What?" Tommy Amundsen burst out. "How can you say
that?"

"Because it's true," I went on. "We have excluded Ted
almost from the very beginning. Rather than helping him,
pulling him along with us, we've gotten mad at him, we've

treated him badly, we have not made him a part of our unit. Last night was a perfect example . . . every single one of us should have volunteered to take the punishment. Because that's what a brother does; he steps in and takes care of his brother. And I believe that if the rest of us had volunteered—none of us would have been punished. Ted didn't answer the questions properly—but the rest of us failed afterwards, and we have failed Ted all semester."

And that's when the whistle blew, and everyone grabbed their bricks and went scrambling out of the chapter room. I tried to move as quickly as I could, but I still couldn't walk as fast, and I felt terrible—knowing they were all going to have to hold the wall till I got there.

The last person out of the room before me was Ted. "Fuck you," he hissed at me as he elbowed me out of the way. "Thanks a fucking lot."

I was stunned. That was the thanks I got? For having my ass beaten to a pulp so I could barely walk? For standing up for him with the rest of the class and pointing out how wrong we'd been treating him? *Well, fuck you too, Ted. You're on your own from now on.*

Despite my protests, I was excused from the wall for the rest of the night, and I also wasn't allowed to participate in anything, and was even allowed to go to sleep at eleven o'clock. But when I woke up on Wednesday morning, the soreness was pretty much gone, and I reported to the wall at the seven A.M. whistle.

There were times Wednesday night when I wished I'd taken the Brotherhood up on their offer to take it easy on me. By the time we were done at three A.M., my body ached with exhaustion, and I was grateful to sink down on the floor with my pillow.

"I'll be down to wake you all in a few hours—around five," Marc said with a smile. "Nice job, guys. Tomorrow morning you need to clean the chapter room—it has to look like you were never here. If you see a brother on campus to-morrow—you cannot speak to him. Tomorrow night, you must be dressed up and lined up underneath the basketball hoop. In a paper bag, you have to have your pledge uni-form. Congratulations, guys, on making it through the week."

By six in the morning I was curled up in my own bed, completely exhausted. I slept until three—screw class, I decided to take the day off, and at promptly six P.M., I was lined up underneath the basketball hoop with my pledge brothers.

"What do you think tonight is all about?" Eric whispered. "We're not going to be initiated until tomorrow night."

I shrugged. "Final test, maybe?"

Marc walked out of the house and across the parking lot toward us, probably for the last time. "Good evening, guys." He gave us his broadest smile. "I am sure you are all wondering what is in store for you tonight." He took a deep breath. "Tonight, you are to meet with the National Exam-iner for Beta Kappa fraternity. He has the final say as to whether you are Beta Kappa material or not. So it's very im-portant that you treat him with respect, answer his ques-tions, and remember—this is the final test for you all. Now, single file follow me into the house one last time."

So, carrying our bags, we followed Marc into the house and into the Great Room one last time. He lined us up against the wall again, and the entire Brotherhood was gath-ered there, solemn looks on their faces. The room was dead silent.

"So, pledges, do you know what tonight is?" Marc asked in a calm and reasonable voice.

No one answered.

"Not one of you knows?"

We glanced at each other puzzled.

"It's fucking Hell Night!" he screamed. "Get into your pledge uniforms RIGHT THE FUCK NOW!"

And the Brotherhood started screaming at us, came right up into our faces. Bewildered, I took off my tie as two brothers screamed into each ear. Blair winked at me, and said, "Put your clothes into the bag," he told me, and as I got each garment off I just shoved it into the bag. I was shaking, I couldn't stand having people yelling at me. I fumbled out of my clothes and put on the filthy stinking clothes I'd worn all week. And then, just as suddenly as it started, the yelling stopped.

"Big brothers," Marc intoned solemnly, "remove a sock from the bag."

They all did.

"Tie it around their left hand."

Blair stepped forward and knotted the sock tightly around my left hand.

"Pledges, the sock is now your pledge pin. You cannot let anyone take it away from you. If someone gets your sock, you are finished at Beta Kappa. Do you understand me?"

"SIR! YES SIR!" we shouted back in unison.

"Big brothers, blindfold them." Blair tied a blindfold over my eyes. "Pledges, turn to your left and put your right hand on your pledge brother's right shoulder." I put my hand up on Ted's shoulder, and felt Chris's hand on me. "DO NOT LET GO OF YOUR BROTHER! No matter what, you must not let go of your pledge brother. Do you understand me?"

"SIR! YES SIR!"

"Forward march!"

We were led outside. I could see nothing, but knew we were outside because I could smell the grass and feel the wind. As we stood there, someone commanded that we sing the fraternity song, so we started singing in low voices. I don't know how long we stood there, but after we finished singing, brothers would move up and down the line. They would try to pull my hand off Ted's shoulder, or Chris's off mine. Others tried to take away my sock, so I finally crossed my arm and tucked it into my right armpit. "All right, pledges," I recognized Marc's voice, "you are about to be led on a journey. You must hold on to your pledge brother. When you reach the end of the journey, I will tell you to let go. Until then, YOU CANNOT LET GO! Do you understand me?"

"SIR! YES SIR!"

And we started moving. They were leading us in a serpentine pattern through the parking lot, and then we went back inside. Once we were inside, it sounded like we had entered the bowels of hell. That horrible tuneless noise made the hairs on the back of my neck stand up. They led us through the house, up a staircase, down a staircase and around and around. Finally, we were led into what had to be the Great Room, and that noise was even louder. Marc whispered into my ear, "Let go," and I dropped my hand. Someone else grabbed my hand, led me somewhere, and then spun me around three times. "Sit down," an unidentifiable voice whispered, and I did.

I don't know how long I sat there on the cold floor. Every so often, someone would grab my sock and try to get it away from me, but I held on doggedly. No one was getting the damned thing away from me.

Finally, someone whispered into my ear, "Stand up." I did, and they took the hand without the sock, and started leading me somewhere. I heard three knocks on a door, and a voice called, "Enter." I heard the door swing open, and the person who was leading me said, "I have another candidate for membership in the Brotherhood here."

"Can you recite the Greek alphabet?" I thought it was Jerry Pollard's voice asking.

"Alpha, beta, gamma, delta, epsilon—"

"Too slow! Get this maggot out of my sight!"

Stunned, I was led out of the room down the hall. Again, the three knocks, again the pronouncement "I have another candidate for membership in the Brotherhood here."

"Do you know the year Beta Kappa was founded?"

I relaxed. I knew this. "Beta Kappa was founded at the Univer—"

"I don't need a fucking history lesson! Get him out of here!"

I was led back into the Great Room and told to sit. Again, I have no idea how long I sat there. It seemed like hours. Then, someone tapped me on the shoulder and told me to stand up. I was led to another door, where again there were the three knocks, the pronouncement, and I was led into a room thick with cigar smoke. I was seated in a chair. I could tell there was more than one other person in the room, but I couldn't tell who they were, or how many there were. I sat there in silence.

"So, you're Jeff Morgan. The brothers have told me a lot about you." A deep, gruff voice said.

"Sir, yes sir!"

"Do you know who I am, maggot?"

"You're the National Examiner, sir!"

"You're goddamned right I am." I heard the sound of a glass filling with liquid, and he drank something. I thought I smelled Scotch when he leaned close to me. "I suppose you think you're hot shit, don't you, boy?"

"Sir, no sir!"

"Always knew your lessons, did what was expected, even took a beating for one of your pledge brothers." He went on in a reasonable voice. "Very, very commendable."

"Sir, thank you, sir." I let out a breath. This wasn't going to be so bad.

"I DON'T GIVE A FUCK WHAT YOU THINK PLEDGE! IT DOESN'T MATTER WHAT THE FUCK-ING BROTHERHOOD THINKS! I AM THE ONLY PERSON WHO DECIDES WHO HAS WHAT IT TAKES TO BE A BROTHER OF BETA KAPPA!" he screamed at me, spittle flying into my face.

Stunned, I opened my mouth and nothing came out.

"Do you like girls?" he asked, again in the reasonable voice.

"Um, yes."

"That didn't sound convincing," he sneered. "You like boys, don't you?" I heard some smothered laughs from around the room.

I didn't answer.

"Answer me, maggot!"

I was shaking by this point. *Fuck the Brotherhood, fuck the brothers, fuck Blair, fuck all of them.* "Fuck you."

The room fell silent.

"Get him out of my sight," The National Examiner said, and someone grabbed my hand and led me back into the Great Room.

I sat there, trembling. I felt like crying. *Why didn't you just say no? You told the National Examiner to fuck off, Like he's going to let you in now. All this energy, all this time, this whole week—you just threw it all away and for what?*

I sat there in my misery forever before someone came and tapped me on the shoulder again. I was led, again the three knocks, and then a door opened. I was led through the doorway, and the door shut behind me.

Someone pulled my blindfold up, and I blinked as I saw Blair. His face looked completely miserable. The entire Brotherhood was inside the Chapter Room, it seemed, and they all looked solemn. I took it all in a second, and then Blair said, his voice shaking, "Jeff, I'm so sorry. The National Examiner said no."

My heart sank to my feet.

"But you know, Jeff, we've all been talking and we all like you and think he's full of shit," Marc Kearney said. "We really want you to be a Beta Kappa, and on behalf of all the brothers, I want to invite you back to pledge again next semester."

I stared at him. I looked around at all the sad, solemn faces. I couldn't believe this was happening. And they thought I would be willing to go through this all again? Oh, hell, no. All I wanted to do was get out of the house as fast as I could run. I looked down and took a deep breath. *Tell them yes, and then get out of here. It's not binding, it'll make them feel okay, but there's no way I am going through this again.* Staring at the rug, I said finally, "Okay."

"Um, Jeff?" Blair said.

I looked into his sad face, and suddenly it split into a joyful smile. "Congratulations, you just passed the final test. Welcome to Beta Kappa!"

My jaw dropped as everyone in the room started cheering. Blair threw his arms around me and hugged me, and my entire body sagged from the shock. Brothers were clapping me on the back, shaking my hand, and then Marc whispered, "You need to go in the back room and keep quiet—we have to bring the rest of your pledge class in." I made my way to the back of the room, and right at the door to the storage room stood a big man in a suit with a mustache and sideburns. He was grinning broadly as he handed me a bottle of champagne. "Congratulations, Jeff." I recognized his voice as the National Examiner.

"You asshole," I said with a huge smile.

"Fuck you, too." He winked, and opened the door. I slid through and my pledge brothers were hugging me. "They are such fucks, huh?" Chris whispered to me, a big grin on his face.

"Uh-huh." I nodded.

"I know, huh?" Eric whispered. "I said I'd come back, but I was thinking, no fucking way!"

"Oh my God, I was thinking the same thing!"

A loud cheer went up from the room outside, and a few seconds later Ted Norris was let into the room. I made a point of hugging him. "We did it, Ted!"

He was stiff, and didn't hug me back.

I let go and stepped away from him. I looked into his face, and saw nothing but malice in his eyes.

Nothing can change him, I thought sadly. *Even tonight, when we've all finally made it, he can't let go.*

There was another cheer, and the door opened. "Come on, boys, let's celebrate!" The so-called National Examiner shouted into the storage room, and we all crowded out into the chapter room, and then out into the Great Room. There was the sound of champagne corks popping, and I drank out of my bottle.

"I'm so proud of you," Blair smiled at me, and I passed him the bottle. He took a big foamy sip and then Marc was ushering us all out into the cul-de-sac. "New brothers, step forward!"

We all stepped to the front of the circle. "Get those fucking shirts off!"

The brothers cheered as we all stripped off the stinky T-shirts and threw them into a pile. Marc doused them with lighter fluid, and lit a match. Suddenly, everyone linked arms and started singing the house song.

> *"It is to thee dear old Beta K, we sing our song of praise,*
> *It is to thee, our fraternity, that we our voices raise!"*

In the sorority parking lots, horns started honking and headlights went on. We all waved in their general direction.

I looked around at my brothers—all of them now my brothers, and felt proud.

I'd made it. We'd all made it.

I took another drink of champagne, and knew I was going to get very wasted.

"I love you," Blair whispered into my ear.

"I'm going to show just how much later, big bro." I smiled back at him. "Prepare to get fucked like you've never been fucked."

"Oh, I know." He laughed. "I've never been fucked by a *brother*. And I can't wait." He brushed up against my shoulder. "I'm sure it's going to be well worth the wait."

PART THREE

WINTER

Chapter 10

The rest of the fall semester went by in a blur. Within two weeks of Initiation, finals began. My grades were pretty much well below the average my parents expected of me after being a straight-A student all through public school. Getting all Cs my first semester of college was, I feared, going to finally make them cross over the line and make me get a job. They'd been pretty patient and understanding about the whole pledging thing, but having substandard grades was unacceptable in my family. Mom and Dad had always taken great pride in my straight As. I'd never let them down before, and now with them paying for my education, I was about to give them the biggest letdown of my life so far.

And worse yet, they might not let me move into the house.

Moving in was now my biggest priority. I wanted to live in the house, to stay there every day, to completely immerse myself in Beta Kappa. I loved the Brotherhood, and was very proud that I'd made it through, been accepted. That meant more to me than getting good grades in a major I didn't care anything about.

After Initiation, I started going over the conversation I was going to have to have with my father about moving in. I came up with every conceivable argument against it that my father could have, and sometimes my answers to those objections sounded phony even to me. But then again, when I'd decided to pledge, and discussed it with them, I'd given them the information packet about Beta Kappa, its requirements, and costs. I knew they'd read it and talked it over. So, they had to know that the Brotherhood required every initiated brother to live in the house a minimum of two semesters.

I rehearsed and thought hard about my answers. The only objection I couldn't come up with an answer for was "You're too young to move out of the house."

And if I knew my mother at all, she was going to say that. The key was to get Dad on my side and present a united front to her.

Finally, the weekend after the Initiation ceremony, I steeled my nerve and sat down with my father to have the talk.

My parents have always been fairly cool with me; I've always been pretty free to do as I chose as long as what few rules they actually set up for me were obeyed. When I was in high school, I never broke the curfew they'd set—not that there was ever any reason to—and I studied and made good grades. They'd been incredibly cool about me joining Beta Kappa—and had never said a word about all the time I'd spent over there during the semester. They'd always been supportive of me. They'd never missed a football or baseball game of mine throughout high school—and at some baseball games, they were the only people in the stands. The other kids envied me my parents, who laughed and joked with them and talked to them like adults. Kevin Hansen had always loved sitting down with my parents after a football game and talking about it. Dad remembered every play, every hit and every tackle. He'd been a three-sport letterman in high school himself—Mom had been head cheerleader—and he was proud that I was a jock too. I remember one time my senior year when I sacked the Olpe High quarterback I could hear my dad screaming above all the other cheers, "Way to go son! That's my son!" And I'd been so happy my eyes filled with tears and I looked for his face in the bleachers and pumped my fist at him. Mom told me later that when I did that a tear ran down his face. They were the best parents I could have hoped for.

Granted, they were devout Church of Christ attendees—twice on Sundays and every Wednesday night. But after I graduated from high school, my attendance was no longer mandatory. I wasn't sure how they'd feel about me being gay though. The Church of Christ was pretty clear on that. It was kind of mercenary of me, but I figured I'd wait until I had my college degree before I had *that* conversation with them.

Well, that wasn't entirely true. I was afraid they would turn their backs on me, disappointed.

And that would break my heart.

"Hey, Dad," I said, sitting on the couch. He was watching the Colts and the Saints play on television. He always rooted for the Saints, since they were perennial underdogs. Dad was like that—but interestingly enough, if one of those underdogs became a winner, he'd stick with them through that first season. But if they kept winning after that, he'd lose interest and start rooting for another underdog. It was one of those weird little things about him I thought was cool.

"Hello, stranger." He gave me a smile. My dad was only thirty-nine, and his hair was still black, with just a hint of gray starting at the temples. Everyone always said that I looked just like him, even though I got my coloring from my mother. "We haven't seen much of you around here in a while. But we figured that was going to happen when you started college," he turned the sound down with a flick of the remote. "You know, son, I don't think I've told you how proud we both are of you."

"Proud? About what?"

"It wasn't easy for you to move away from your friends and all your plans and start your life over again." He smiled at me. "And you've never complained once."

"Well, it was hard," I admitted. "And I wasn't really happy about it, but you know, it worked out for the best. I'm really happy here."

"Life has a funny way of working out sometimes, doesn't it?" he said, popping some peanuts in his mouth. "We've missed having you around, though."

"I know," I said, steeling my nerve. "Between my duties at the fraternity and studying, I've been pretty busy." I felt myself start to color as I lied about studying, and thought, *I really need to buckle down.*

He gave me a look. "Well, son, your mother and I were talking the other night, and we know you're going to want to move into the frat house."

I bit my lip. I could hardly say to my father what had been drilled into my head all semester: *Don't call it a 'frat.' You wouldn't call your country a 'cunt', would you?*

"Obviously, we would much rather you stay living here

with us. You're our only child, but you're not a little boy anymore and you have your own life to live. And we can understand that. You can't live here with us forever, much as we would like you to," he went on. "And if we'd stayed in Kansas, you would have moved into one of the dorms at Kansas State, right? So you'd already be gone. We talked it over and decided that we can afford to pay your rent there at the house, according to that cost sheet you gave us when you first joined. But we are placing some conditions on that. First of all, you have to maintain a B average the entire time you are living there. If you ever drop below that, you are moving back in here—no questions, no arguments. Understood?" I nodded. "Second, for this next semester we'll help you out with spending money, but next summer you have to get a job and save for the upcoming school year. You need to start learning some financial responsibility. If you're old enough to not live under our roof, you're old enough to learn the value of hard work and a dollar. Is that understood?"

"Yes." I wanted to jump up and dance around the room. Instead, I kept a serious expression on my face. "Um, Dad, about this semester—"

"C average is all we're expecting from you, Jeff." My relief must have shown in my face because he laughed. "Transitioning from high school to college is hard, and you made an even bigger transition. We understand that, and we know the frat kept you hopping. But you're too smart to get Cs, and without the pledging distractions, we expect you to really apply yourself."

"Thanks, Dad," I replied. I was flying high. It was going so much better than I could have hoped. I took a deep breath and went on, "Um, do you think it would be possible for me to move into the house right after finals?"

"Why so soon?" He looked a little stricken. "What's the rush?"

I explained that Beta Kappa had a rule about room seniority. Since the house usually emptied out for summer and Christmas vacations, any brother willing to stay in the house during those times was entitled to have his own room when school reconvened. It was how Blair managed to get his own room, by staying through the summer session. He'd had to share as a junior active the semester before, and it had nearly driven him insane. "No offense, Jeff, you know I love you but if we share a room we'll be at each other's throats within days. These rooms are too small—at least for me to share one. After you live in for a year we'll get an apartment together. But if you move in over Christmas, you'll earn more seniority than guys who stay in the summer." This was because everyone went home over Christmas—there were no Christmas classes, like there were in the summer—and it was really convenient for me because my parents actually lived in Polk.

"And I think it will be easier for me to get good grades if I don't have a roommate. You know, that way I can have quiet time to study," I concluded. The real reason I wanted my own room was because no roommate meant no extra pair of eyes watching me and Blair in private.

If Blair couldn't share a room with me, I didn't want to live with anyone else. And how horrible would it be to have the Brotherhood stick me with someone like Ted Norris?

I couldn't even think about that.

"Well, son, that makes a lot of sense." My dad smiled at me and shook his head. "Sounds like you've got it all figured out. When did you grow up and get so smart?"

I just smiled. I impulsively gave him a big hug. "I love you, Dad."

So the next few weeks were spent in a flurry of studying and writing papers. Blair was just as crazed as I was—his average had slipped over the semester as well, so we were both trying to catch up. I talked to my instructors, got advice, and studied everything over and over again until it seemed like at night I dreamed about my classes.

Talk about nightmares!

But it paid off. All of my papers got As—which wasn't a big surprise; I've always been good at writing papers—and every single final I took I breezed through. There was not a single question on any test that I didn't know the answer to—at least, thought I knew the answer to, which was a very good feeling and very different from my experiences earlier in the semester.

I was actually able to move into my room on the second to last day of finals. Mine were over on Wednesday, and I was moving into Danny Fisher's room. Danny had taken his finals early because his family was spending Christmas in Paris, and he was moving into an apartment when he returned. My parents got me one of those small refrigerators, a new single bed, and a microwave as my Christmas presents—Danny had left his desk behind for me to use. It didn't really take that long to set up my room—although my mom cried when I left the house with the last load I was taking, which in turn made me cry. "It's not like I'm going that far away," I said, wiping my eyes. "I'm just about ten minutes away."

"But you won't be under my roof anymore," she sobbed. "You'd better come home to visit every week!"

When I pulled away from my parents' house, it really hit me. *I'm moving out, I'm going to live on my own.*

It was a small step toward adulthood and away from being a child.

By the time I got to the house, the parking lot was pretty much emptied out. The brothers weren't sticking around for long once they were finished—they were loading up their cars and heading home. I hugged Marc Kearney good-bye as he put the last load of what he was taking home with him in the back of his battered old white pick-up. "Have a great Christmas, Marc," I said when we broke apart.

"Yeah, you too." He gave me his big smile. "You're going to love living in the house, bro. It's a whole different world for you now."

"Yeah." I waved as he started the truck and pulled out of the parking lot. Over at Alpha Xi Delta, I could see the same kind of departure scenes going on. I grabbed a box and headed inside. I was kind of bummed that my room was upstairs—I'd wanted to be as close to Blair as possible, but that just hadn't worked out. I lugged the box up the back staircase and stood for a moment in front of the door to room seventeen. I put the key in, unlocked the door, and dragged the box in. My bed was covered with boxes and bags of clothes. I stood there for a moment, then walked over to the window and opened the curtains and looked out over the backyard. This was going to be my home for the next year. I planned on staying in the house over the summer, and then after next fall semester ended, Blair and I would get our own apartment somewhere. We hadn't talked about where it would be, but I knew it wouldn't be in the Valencia. Blair hated that place.

There was a wrapped box sitting on top of my desk next

to my laptop. I walked over and sat down. I picked it up and opened the card. In big red letters on a white background it read *Congratulations!* Smiling to myself, I opened the card and started reading.

Jeff,

Welcome to Beta Kappa! Knowing you has been one of the greatest things to ever happen to me in my life. We're going to have so many good times in the future—but for now, here's a moving in gift for you.

Love,
Blair

I tore open the box and started laughing.

My housewarming gift was a glass bong, screens, and a big bag of pot.

So, of course, I had to try it all out before I started unpacking.

It was *very* good pot. It took me much longer to unpack than it probably should have.

When Blair was finished studying for his final the next day, he came up to my room and we got stoned—and broke in my bed.

And if I do say so myself, it was the best sex we'd had to date.

I'm not sure why that was—maybe it was because we'd had so little time to be together over the past few weeks. Maybe it was because we both knew we'd be apart for at least three weeks. Whatever the reason, Blair and I couldn't get enough of each other. When we finally collapsed, spent and exhausted, we were both drenched in sweat and within a few moments, we were both sound asleep, our bodies entwined.

By Saturday morning, Blair and I were the only brothers left in the house, which was kind of fun. Originally, I wasn't going to be the only brother living in the house over Christmas break, but the other two—Jerry Pollard and Randy Pritchard, changed their minds and went home as well. Saturday morning, we made sure every door in the house was locked, the curtains in the Great Room were closed, and I fucked him there on the carpet. We did it again in the communal shower on the second floor. "It's kind of fun doing it in places we never in a million years would dare to, huh?" Blair said with a grin after he shot a big load that washed down the shower drain.

"You know it," I said, pulling his body to me and kissing him deep and hard.

Around one, though, it was time for him to get going as well. "I hate leaving you here by yourself," he said as he dressed. "I'm going to miss you so much."

"I hate you leaving me here by myself." I was sitting on his bed, naked. "Call me every day?"

"You know it." He came over and kissed me on the lips. "And besides, you won't be here by yourself all that long." It was true. The spring semester officially started on January 15th, but every year everyone came back for New Year's, and the house threw a massive party to celebrate not only the coming of the new year, but the end of the previous semester. "Are you sure you don't want to come with me? We'd have so much fun."

"My parents would never in a million years let me go away for Christmas. Besides, I'm in charge of the house while everyone is gone." It wasn't really much responsibility, frankly. I just had to make sure the place didn't burn down or get broken into.

"Well, why don't you come down right after Christmas for a few days?" He asked. "We could go to my dad's place out in Palm Springs. You'll love Palm Springs. It's wonderful there."

"Okay, let me think about it." I started putting on my clothes so I could walk him out to the car. "But I'd have to be back in time for the New Year's party."

"I told you I wouldn't miss that party for the world." Blair gave me a mock glare. "If I didn't know better, I'd think you weren't going to miss me at all."

"Now you're just being silly." I smiled. Things between us had changed a bit since the blowup over Marc Kearney. In a way, my intense need for him had lessened. I didn't love him any less, but I'd realized in that two day period when I thought I had lost him forever that I needed to rein it in a bit. It wasn't that I loved him less, nor was it that I desired him any less. But the truth was, as I realized during the weeks that followed that speed bump in our relationship, that I had no real control over what happened with the two of us. I loved him, but had slept with Marc without even a second thought other than shooting a load inside his ass. If I could do that, there was no reason why Blair couldn't as well—and we'd even discussed the possibilities of it happening during our separation. And while neither one of us liked the idea, we had come to the conclusion that if it happened, it happened—and it didn't mean we cared for each other any less. "You know I'm going to miss you."

He gave me a big hug and kiss, and I walked him out to the car. It was cold and gray outside, and a damp wind was blowing that seemed to go right through my skin into my bones. I watched him drive off, waving until his car made the turn off the cul-de-sac and was out of sight. I walked back into the empty house. It was weird how silent it was. Even during the mandatory weeknight quiet hours (which started at seven P.M.) there was always some noise in the house. But now the whole place was silent as a tomb, other than the sound of the wind rushing around the house. The house was also cold and drafty. I shivered a bit as I went back into my room and turned on the space heater. What I really wanted to do with all the solitude was write.

The days passed, and I became more and more used to being alone in the house. Every so often I would go over to my parents' for dinner, but most of the time I didn't like to leave the house. I was taking a creative writing course the next semester which required me to write four short stories, and Jerry Pollard had offered to read and critique the stories for me—so I wanted to get drafts of them finished over the Christmas break.

And being alone in the house allowed me to do other things as well. Blair had left some porn DVD's for me to "entertain" myself with, and rather than watching them in the privacy of his room, I chose to watch them in the Great Room, naked, and pleasure myself in there. I sometimes would beat off in the communal showers quite happily.

In fact, I found that most of the time I was walking around the house either naked or in my underwear. It was kind of cool.

It was about eight o'clock on Christmas Eve when I walked naked to the showers. I'd spent most of the day at my parents', but had come back to the house around six. They'd wanted me to sleep over, but I begged off, promising to come back early the next morning and spend the day with them.

I was very pleasantly stoned, and my dick was hard. I was going to beat off again under the hot spray with my cock nice and soapy. My towel was draped over my shoulder when someone called my name.

After my heart started beating at a normal pace, my breathing was more regular, and I'd had a moment to wrap my towel around my waist and start willing my erection away, I said, "Jesus, Kenny! You scared me to death!"

"Hated the thought of you here all alone, buddy." Kenny Frame was one of the few brothers I didn't know well, because he didn't live in the house. As he walked up to me, grinning, I realized with horror that not only was I alone in the house with him, I was already hard and practically naked. He punched me in the shoulder, hard enough to force me to take a step backward.

Kenny was a local, an honest to God, born and raised here native of Polk, California. He'd lived in the house for three years, and had moved out at the beginning of the previous summer, getting an apartment with a non-brother. He was a big guy, about six four and two hundred thirty pounds of solid muscle. He'd played on the CSUP football team on an athletic scholarship his first two years in school, but he liked to party a little too much so he'd quit. He had a mop of unruly curly reddish blond hair, freckles across his nose, brown eyes and a body that was all veined muscle. I'd hung out with him a few times, and liked him. He had an odd sense of humor, and sometimes went a little too far with the teasing, but he was always grinning and in a good mood, and never meant anything by it. Kenny wasn't popular with the majority of the brothers, especially with the Executive

Council. When he got drunk, so the stories went, he had a tendency to do crazy things, and would become belligerent when anyone tried to interfere. I'd heard it had taken four of the biggest guys in the house to restrain him once. Another time he'd gotten drunk, gone out into the parking lot, and started hitting golf balls in the direction of the Alpha Xi Delta house. Several shattered car windows later, someone had managed to get the golf club away from him and put him to bed.

Obviously, relations with the sisters of Alpha Xi were a little strained for a while after that.

"What about your family?" My dick was shrinking, thank God.

He shrugged. "They're sitting around watching *It's a Wonderful Life* and in about another hour or two, they'll be asleep. I knew you were here, and I felt like partying." Out of one of his jacket pockets he pulled a bottle of Jose Cuervo Gold. Out of the other he pulled out a bag of white powder. "You've got pot, don't you?"

"Yeah, of course I do."

He grinned at me. "Go ahead and take your shower, and I'll wait for you in your room."

"Um, okay. The room's open." I stood there like a fool and watched him walk up the hallway to my room. He was so fucking hot. His legs were all thick muscle, and he had this great big muscular ass that strained against his jeans as though trying to break out. I'd partied with Kenny before— but never alone. It would be so tempting, I thought as I soaped up my body in the shower, to try something, but I wouldn't, couldn't. Kenny was cool, but he wasn't that cool—and besides, he could kick my ass with one arm tied behind his back. And if he was drunk—and there was no one around to talk him down—the thought made me shudder. Yeah, no matter how fucked up I got, I'd have to keep my hands to myself. I got under the spray of hot water and took my shower.

My towel tied securely around my waist, I walked back into my room. He'd put an old Fleetwood Mac CD on my stereo, and two fat lines of coke were already laid out on my framed picture of Blair and me from Initiation Night. Two shot glasses filled with golden liquor were set out on my desk, and Kenny was finishing the last remnants of ash and pot in my bong. He grinned at me as I pulled on a pair of sweatpants. He held the bong out to me. "Refill, please," he said in a childlike voice that made me think of *Oliver Twist*: "may I have some more, sir?"

I sat down at my desk and got out the tin I kept my pot in, tearing some pieces off a damp bud with purplish red hairs growing out of it. I lit up, inhaling, listening to the water bubble inside the glass, letting go of the vent hole and letting the cooled smoke fill my lungs before passing it back to him. He did the same as I blew out a stream of smoke that seemed to fill my little room. Somehow, the room seemed even smaller with him sitting on my bed. Kenny let out his hit, coughing a little, then passed the bong back to me. I gestured for him to keep it, and he took two more hits.

"Damn," he said, his eyes watering as he put the bong down. "That's good grass, man."

I shrugged and took the tequila glass he offered. We clinked the glasses together and tossed the liquor back. It was smooth, but strong, and the burning didn't start until it was all the way down. Then came the lines of coke. I hadn't done coke since the night with Marc—and I wondered if doing it again was a sign of possibilities to come. I tried not to be too obvious as I snuck glances over at Kenny. Damn, he filled out those jeans really nicely. *Stop that! Are you crazy?* I reminded myself. *He can break you in half with one hand. Just don't go there—don't even fucking think about it.*

After some more bong hits, another line of coke and a couple more shots of the tequila, I was feeling pretty fucked up. Kenny was still sitting on the side of my bed and I was in my desk chair. We talked about little things—brothers we liked, brothers we didn't like, wasn't that a great party, and so on. I kept sneaking glances over at him out of the corner of my eyes.

He really had the most amazing body.

After a fourth shot, I decided I needed to stop with the tequila. I was getting too drunk, and I was afraid that I might not be able to trust myself to be around him. It had been two weeks since Blair had gone home—and even though we talked on the phone every day and e-mailed each other dozens of times, I missed the feel of another man in my arms. No matter how many times I beat off, it just wasn't the same. And Kenny was sexy as hell.

Kenny just grinned, pouring himself another shot. "Yeah, best to pace yourself, I always say." He threw the shot back like it was the first, making a loud "ah" sound and putting the glass down. "I feel pretty good." He stretched his arms up overhead, and I could see the big lat muscles fanning out underneath his sweater. "Too bad no chicks around." He winked at me.

"Yeah." I tried to sound enthusiastic. I was starting to sweat a little.

He grabbed his crotch and rubbed it. "Tequila and coke always make me horny, ya know?"

"Uh-huh." My mind was racing through its fog. The tequila had soaked in, and the pot wasn't helping much, although the coke had me completely alert. It was a weird combination, one I wasn't sure I liked very much. And I wasn't entirely comfortable with the direction this conversation was heading. *Don't even think he is going there for one second*, I told myself, *because he isn't. Kenny Frame is into women, and women only. Keep your hands off and remember that. This is where you could get yourself into some serious, major trouble.*

"You don't get laid much, do you?" Kenny was looking at me seriously. "I mean, I don't think I've ever heard of you banging one chick all semester."

This wasn't the first time this had come up with one of the brothers. I shrugged, giving my standard response. "I just don't see much need to brag about it." This often had the desired effect; implying that brothers who bragged didn't get much action—which usually made the person who brought it up in the first place redden and shut up.

"I don't buy it." Kenny winked at me. "Me, I think you like guys."

My jaw dropped. *Oh, fuck.* Through my fogged mind, I tried to figure out an appropriate response. "I do not!" I squeaked out finally and cursed at myself. *Yeah, that sounded masculine and convincing. Nice move!*

"You sure?" Kenny gave me that big grin again. "Some of the other brothers think so."

The tequila churned in my stomach, just as a big drip of coke went down my throat. I gagged, horrified, not knowing what to say, what to do. Blair and I had always been so careful. We knew that not ever hooking up very publicly with any girls was a risk—especially since we spent so much time together. Chris and Eric were very publicly heterosexual, even though I suspected they really weren't as "bisexual" as they'd told me. Blair and I had never once talked about what might happen if people started talking about us in that way. Fuck! I wanted the world to collapse then, wanted a big hole in the floor to open up and suck me down. "Who?" I managed to keep my voice steady. "Who's said that about me?"

"Nobody who matters, really." Kenny poured himself another shot of tequila. "Assholes nobody likes, nobody listens to. I don't care, myself."

"Huh?" I couldn't do anything but stare at him. My mind was racing a million miles an hour. *Who is saying that shit about me? Are they saying it about Blair too? What the hell are we going to do?*

"Don't matter to me," he went on as though I hadn't spoken. "You get your rocks off how you get your rocks off, ya know? I don't give a shit. Hell, I've done it a couple of times myself."

"You have?" I couldn't quite believe what I was hearing. Kenny Frame, the big muscle stud football player who fucked any chick who even looked at him sideways? It had to be the tequila. I reached for the bong with shaking hands and took another hit.

"Everyone has." He looked at me. "Anyone who says they never have is a fucking liar." He smiled. "I mean, come on, Jeff. Haven't you?"

"No. No, I never have."

"Really?" he shrugged. "Okay, man, if you say so." He measured out two more lines of coke. "Damn, it's hot in here." He passed me the picture frame. As I took the rolled up dollar bill and started to inhale my line, he pulled the sweater up over his head.

This can't be happening, I thought to myself as I tried not to look at his body. He was all smooth, tanned thick muscle. Big hard round pecs with half-dollar-sized purple nipples, a completely flat hard stomach with a trail of hair leading from the navel to the waist of his tight jeans. His arms were big, solid, thick, and strong. My dick was getting hard, in spite of myself.

He laughed. "You're getting a boner, just thinking about it. Aren't you?" He winked at me.

I crossed my legs, passing the frame back. I didn't say anything. I couldn't. My mind was racing, my coked-up blood pumping into my dick.

He did his line and put the frame down, kicking off his shoes. He stood up and undid the button fly of his jeans and then peeled them off his powerful legs, standing before me in just his white briefs. He had a hard-on, too. He got back onto the bed, kneeling in the middle of the mattress. "Let's wrestle." He growled. "I've got some energy I need to burn off."

I laughed, but it sounded choked and forced to me. "Like that would be fair. You'd kick my ass in two seconds." But the thought of having that body wrapped around mine was enticing.

"You chicken?" he taunted, flexing his big arms.

"Well, yeah. I mean, you could kill me without even trying."

He laughed, delighted. "You should be chicken. I knew you were a smart guy." He winked at me. "Aw, come on, I won't hurt you, Jeff. That wouldn't be any fun. Of course I'll win, but it's the struggle that's fun, you know? Two men tussling together to see who's the strongest? Don't you think that's hot, Jeff? You know you do."

"I don't think it's such a good idea." I shook my head. "Seriously, man." I forced out a laugh. "I mean, Kenny. It's kind of weird, don't you think?"

"What's weird is why you have such a problem with having a friendly wrestling match with one of your brothers." He climbed off the bed and walked over to my dresser, pulling out the top drawer and pulling out a pair of pale blue underwear Blair had given me. They were bikini cut, which he liked to see me in, saying "It always reminds me of you in my red bikini next to Dad's pool, sexy as hell but shy and nervous with no idea of just the affect you were having on everyone around you." Kenny held them up and grinned. "Very nice," he said with a grin and tossed them to me. "Put those on. It'll be fun, you'll see."

"Kenny, I—"

"If you're worried about getting a hard-on, don't be." He reached down and grabbed his own. "See? I've got one. No big deal, you see?"

I swallowed. It was so tempting. "Um—"

"Come on, man." He was losing patience. "I told you I wouldn't hurt you. Don't be such a pussy. You'll see, it's fun."

I gave up and got to my feet. "All right, already." I dropped my sweatpants and pulled the underwear up and on. "You happy now?"

He hopped back on the bed, the grin back on his face. "This'll be fun, you'll see. And the hard-ons are no big deal. If you watch the Olympic guys, they have hard-ons in their singlets all the time. It's a male thing, you know? Primal."

"Uh-huh." I took a deep breath and climbed up onto the bed. He was about a foot away from me, both of us on our knees.

"You ready?" he asked, a big grin on his face.

I nodded, and he grabbed me.

It took him about twenty seconds to pin me. As I'd thought, I didn't have a chance against him. I couldn't budge him. He outweighed me by too much, and was much stronger. Anything I tried to do was useless . . . whenever I got him into a hold, he could counter it and get me into something much worse. We went a couple more times, him even letting me get him in a hold to start with, but it made absolutely no difference. He could just power out of it and then I was just there for the taking.

My cock was aching. I hadn't been this close to another man physically in weeks, feeling him and his cool, soft, smooth skin on top of me. I tried to burn the memories into my brain, to beat off to later. He was so strong, so powerful, and so masculine. I could smell his armpits, and one time he had me facedown on the bed in a full nelson, his big heavy muscled arms wrapped through mine and behind my head, and he was lying on top of me. I could feel his hard dick on my ass, and I wondered where this would all lead . . . This was great, but even so, it wasn't enough.

I wanted him, God help me. I wanted him inside of me. I wanted to take his cock in my mouth and make him moan and squirm with pleasure.

I was hot with desire.

After the fourth straight time he'd made me cry "uncle," I pushed away from him, sitting back on my pillows while trying to catch my breath. The physical exertion had sobered me up. He was breathing hard too, which I found hard to believe. I couldn't believe I had worn him out . . . and I kept trying not to look at his hard-on, which was even more obvious than before.

"You done?" he panted.

"Well, yeah." I took a deep breath. "I'm fucking exhausted, man."

He held out his right hand for me to shake. "You're a tough little monkey, aren't you?"

"Huh?" I stared at him. He'd made mincemeat out of me. I hadn't been able to do a thing to him.

"Most guys won't even go a second round with me," he said, reaching for the tequila bottle.

"Yeah, well." There wasn't anything else to say. Maybe they didn't like having him on top of them the way I did.

He slid a hand inside of his underwear. "Man, I gotta get this off." He grinned at me. "I should make you suck me off."

Much as I wanted to do it, I knew I couldn't admit it to him. Not then. I backed up against the headboard. "No way."

"I *could* make you."

"Yeah, you probably could," I admitted, which made him laugh.

He grabbed a bottle of lotion off my dresser, and squirted some into his hands before handing it to me. "Come on, buddy, we'll just go ahead and beat off. Beat off buddies, okay?"

Beat off buddies? I shrugged. "Okay."

He slid his underwear down, and sat back on the bed. I gulped and slid my own down, squirting the Jergens onto my own dick. He patted the bed next to him. "Sit here by me."

Naked, I sat down next to him, our legs almost touching. He then took his right leg and placed it over mine. He closed his eyes and started stroking his dick. I sat, stroking myself, watching him, my eyes wandering over his body, wondering how his nipples would taste in my mouth, wondering what his dick would taste like, what it would feel like to . . .

And before I knew it, I came.

He opened his eyes and grinned at me. "You wanna help me out here, bud?"

I nodded.

"Suck on my nipples. That drives me crazy."

I leaned over and took his right nipple into my mouth. I felt his entire body stiffen as I began to suck on it, tease it with my tongue.

"Bite it," he commanded.

I did.

"Harder than that!"

I bit down hard.

He moaned and his entire body went rigid. "Ah, ah, AAAHHHHH!!!" He exploded, and I felt some of it get on my back.

I let go of his nipple and moved away from him.

"Nice job, buddy." He gave me a lazy grin. He grabbed my towel off the floor and wiped himself dry. "I knew I'd have a good time with you."

I didn't say anything. I didn't know what to say. I sat there, naked, my come drying on me, as he got dressed. Once he'd finished tying his shoes, he walked over and leaned into me, and planted a deep kiss on my mouth.

"Till next time, buddy," he whispered, and then walked out of the room.

I sat there for a few minutes, staring at the door, and then reached for my bong.

Next time?

I smiled and took a hit. I heard the door at the foot of the steps slam. I picked up the framed picture. He'd left me some coke, and I took the dollar bill and snorted another line. I wiped up some of the debris and rubbed it on my gums. I took another bong hit, then got back into the bed and thought about what had just happened.

Kenny Frame was the last guy in the house I would have ever expected to have—well, it really wasn't *sex*, after all. How would you describe it? Wrestling between two brothers—jacking off together afterwards, and sucking on his nipples? And being kissed good-bye? I didn't understand any of it, none of it made any sense to me.

In one semester as a brother of Beta Kappa, I'd had some kind of sexual experience with six brothers out of eighty actives. I was in love with my big brother—we had sex together every chance we could grab. I'd had wrestling experiences with Chris and Eric together, and then again with Kenny. All three of them had acted like they would be more than happy to do it again as well. I'd fucked Marc Kearney and blown Rory Armagh.

Out of all of them, Rory was the only one who acted like it never happened.

Surely, there was more of this going on in the house than what I knew about. Blair had intimated on more than one occasion there was a lot of it. What had he said, back last summer?

"Straight boys don't care who get them off when they're fucked up. All they care about is shooting a load, and it doesn't matter whose mouth or hole it's in. If they think about it all when they sober it, they blame the booze or whatever because they're certainly not gay."

Maybe I was being a little too oversensitive. Maybe I

was just stoned or still a little drunk or coked up. But it didn't seem right. Why did Blair and I have to keep what we had a secret from the rest of the Brotherhood?

I thought back to some of the lessons we were taught throughout the pledge semester. *A brother never lies to another brother.*

But every day, Blair and I lied to everyone about who we were. Not to the extreme that Chris and Eric did, or even Marc. Blair and I never tried to get in the pants of girls in front of the other brothers, never tried to prove over and over again that we were so masculine, so straight, that no one would ever suspect we actually were in love with each other, or would rather be with a guy than whatever drunk girl was handy at the moment.

Something was wrong with this picture.

Everything Beta Kappa stood for—its ideals, its creed, and so forth—none of it had anything to do with sexuality. It was all about a moral code—of loyalty to the house, of honesty and integrity, of being a good student and a contributing member of society.

Being in love with Blair did not make any of those things less possible for me. If anything, it had bound me tighter to the Brotherhood.

I took another bong hit, and grabbed my notebook and a pen.

I started writing.

Chapter 11

"Cut! You guys can take a break now, okay?"

I slid my cock out of Chad Revere's ass and squinted over at the director. I couldn't really see him (or was it her? I wasn't really sure) because the sun was directly behind where the others were gathered.

"Can you hand me a cigarette?" Chad asked, rolling over onto his back. Chad wasn't his real name, but I couldn't remember what that was either. I'd met so many people with two names I couldn't keep track of what was real and what wasn't anymore. He was very sexy, with a chiseled, tanned body that was almost completely hairless except for the neatly trimmed pubic hair around his floppy cock. His hair was bleached blond at the tips but dark underneath, and his face was young and innocent looking. His voice was high-pitched and world weary, though, and he spoke with a bit of a lisp. He'd told me before we started the scene that this was his fifteenth video shoot in less than six months. "Dancing and escorting is where the money really is," he'd told me, chain smoking one Marlboro Light after another while we waited for them to set up the scene. "This your first time?"

"Uh-huh." I replied.

"Don't worry about a thing. I'm an old pro—I can get you through it."

Making a porn movie was the last thing in the world I thought I'd be getting myself into when I drove down to Palm Springs in the Flying Couch the day after Christmas. Blair was sitting over with the director and the cameraman somewhere. He'd called me on Christmas, lonely and bored. His father's movie had run over schedule, and he was trapped filming in Australia. "I'm stuck here with nothing but servants," Blair wailed into the phone. "Please tell me you can meet me in Palm Springs tomorrow. Please."

"Okay," I said, "just e-mail me the address so I can Mapquest directions, okay?"

And so, the next morning I threw a suitcase in the trunk of the Flying Couch and headed south out of Polk. It took me about six hours to get there, and when I pulled into the driveway of Steve Blanchard's Palm Springs manse, the white Lexus was already there. I was surprised there was no security gate or anything—given the high tech security of the house in Beverly Hills, the big ranch-style house was pretty open to whoever wanted access to it. The front yard was all sand, with a large cactus here and there, and metal abstract sculptures reflecting the hot sun. I rang the doorbell, and Blair opened the front door just a few moments later. "Thank God you're here!" He flew into my arms, hugging me so tight I could barely breathe. "I was about to slit my wrists."

I laughed, "You're exaggerating." Still, I'd missed him, and luxuriated in the feel of his body against mine. He wasn't wearing a shirt or shoes, just a pair of white cotton tennis shorts with nothing underneath. He'd gotten more tan since he'd left Polk, and I reached down and cupped his hard ass with my hands and squeezed. He hopped up, wrapping his legs around my waist, and I kissed him. My cock responded, despite how tired I was from being in the car for so long, and as his tongue explored my mouth I gently lowered him to the marble floor and pinched his nipples. He gasped and moaned. "Fuck me. Jeff. Right here. I need you so bad." He pulled my T-shirt up over my head and started kissing my chest as I fumbled with my belt. I went up on my knees and pulled my pants down, and he sat up and took me in his mouth. My entire body shivered as he started working my cock with his mouth and tongue. He lapped at my cock like he needed it to survive. With his hands he pushed his own shorts down, and then lay back on the cool floor, spreading his legs for me.

"Fuck me," he pleaded. "Fuck me hard. I need it so bad."

I spit in my hand, rubbed it on my cock and I shoved him backwards. He fell back to the floor and I shoved my cock into him as hard as I could. His lips parted as he cried out, and I drove deep inside of him. "Oh yeah, please, fuck me hard, as rough as you can, please, I need it so bad . . ."

I began pumping him, driving my hips back and forth as violently as I could. With each thrust, his head went back and he gasped. His whole body began to shake, and then he came suddenly, squirting out his load all over his chest. I was close so I kept going, pounding and pounding until I finally came with a shout of my own before collapsing on the floor beside him. He rolled over on top of me, burying his head in my neck. "Mmmm," he whispered. "That's exactly what I needed. God, I've missed you."

"You couldn't find anyone down here?" I asked.

He stiffened in my arms. He pulled away from me and sat up. There was a hurt expression on his face. "What is that supposed to mean, Jeff?" He crossed his arms. "I missed you. I wanted you." He scrambled to his feet. "And I thought you wanted me to. I suppose you've been—oh, never mind."

To my horror, he started to cry.

"Jeff." I pulled my pants up and hugged him from behind. "I'm sorry. I was only kidding. Of course I missed you." I squeezed him. "Is everything okay?"

"I'm sorry." He wiped his face and leaned back into me. "It just sucked being alone on Christmas. Again." He pulled away from me and picked up his shorts. "Come on, let me show you around."

"Do you want to talk about it?" I asked.

He smiled at me. "Not right now. Maybe later." He shook his head. "Follow me."

The house looked small from the driveway, but on the inside it was much bigger. He led me from the foyer into a huge living room with a high ceiling. The floor was the same marble as the foyer; the walls were painted an off white. A small fountain bubbled in one corner of the room, and I saw that it's base drained into a makeshift stream that led outside and emptied into the swimming pool. Over the fireplace was a massive print of Steve Blanchard from his first movie—the one that made him a star. "Wow," I said, walking over to it.

Blair laughed. "Yeah, that's something, isn't it?"

I'd seen *The Pool Boy* at least twenty times myself. Steve Blanchard had been twenty and had played some small roles in a couple of movies when he landed the starring role. The movie had been intended as a comeback vehicle for Denise Moss, an actress in her forties whose career had kind of slid. She played a woman whose husband had just left her for a younger woman, and who is contemplating suicide when she sees a beautiful young man emerging from her swimming pool naked. He turns out to be her new pool boy, and they wind up having sex. She slowly becomes obsessed with him, and at the very end, she shoots him. But when the film debuted, all anyone—critics and audiences alike—could talk about was the incredible beauty of young Steve Blanchard. The scene where he emerges dripping wet out of the pool in slow motion for the first time, is considered one of the great classic scenes in film history. It was a truly amazing shot. The print showed Steve, soaking wet, emerging naked from the pool, water cascading down every muscle.

"It's kind of creepy to come into the living room and see your father naked," Blair went on. "I'm sure someday I'll have a great conversation with a therapist about it."

I shrugged. "It's a great print, but you're right. I don't think I could handle having something like that around of my dad."

"Come on, let's put your suitcase in our room, then we can go sit by the pool and drink some wine." He winked. "And later on, I'll take you over to meet the neighbors. Did you like that porn I left for you?"

"Yeah, it was hot."

"The producer/director has the house next door." He grinned. "And she's shooting a film this weekend. She said we could watch some of the shoot, if we wanted to."

"That could be interesting."

"Might be good material for you to write about someday." Blair laughed. "You never know. Come on, let me show you around."

The house spread out from the living room. The kitchen was to the right, and beyond that was the master bedroom suite. It was incredibly luxurious, with probably the biggest bed I'd ever seen, and mirrors everywhere. And on every wall were prints of Steve Blanchard. Some dressed, some undressed, from every stage of his career. There were framed magazine covers he'd appeared on, everything from *Time* to *Vanity Fair* to *Esquire*. On a dresser sat several People's Choice awards, and the Emmy he'd won for a made-for-TV movie called *Nobody's Hero,* in which he'd played a mentally handicapped man who rescued a baby from a burning building. I walked over and picked it up. It was surprisingly heavy. "This room—"

"I call it the Steve Shrine," Blair said, a bitter tone in his voice. "He has this here, because he only comes out here to relax, you know. He can't have all this in Beverly Hills, because people might think he's an egomaniac—and his gimmick is his humility, you know." He made a gagging noise.

"Blair—" I hesitated. "Is everything okay with you and your dad?"

"Later. I'll tell you all that later, okay? But right now, let me show you the rest of the house."

The other side of the house was where the spare bedrooms were—Blair's room was almost as big as the master bedroom, with its own bathroom. As opposed to the rest of the house, Blair's room was filled with photos and prints of Nicole Blair. There wasn't a single picture of his father. And on the mantel of the fireplace stood an Oscar. "Is that your mother's Oscar?"

"Yeah. She gave it to me." Blair walked over and picked it up. "She doesn't care about things like that. Unlike Dad, *she's* really humble. She does it because she loves the work, not for awards or to be a star. I think that was why their marriage didn't work out—she couldn't stand the whole Hollywood movie star trip Dad's on." He laughed. "But enough about me and my neurotic parents." He jumped on the bed. "Sit down here and tell me all about your Christmas."

I got up on the bed with him and he cuddled into me. I started stroking his hair while I told him about Christmas with my parents. *Something's bothering him, I don't know what, but he's different, something's happened or changed since he left Polk.*

"That sounds nice," Blair said. "Look, I'm sorry, I know I've been acting like I'm crazy ever since you've got here. I've just never had a Christmas like a normal person, you know? This time of year it gets to me, is all. I'm usually okay with things, but at Christmas it bothers me."

Once he started talking, the story started pouring out of him. His parents had gotten divorced when he was barely two years old. One of the conditions of the divorce was that his mother couldn't take him to England—she had to stay in the United States, or she'd lose custody. When she got an offer to make a movie over there, she'd left him with his father and gone. During the making of the movie, she'd fallen in love with and married her costar—his stepfather, Ian Westcombe. Ian had no interest in living in California. "So, she chose her new husband over me," Blair said bitterly. "Don't get me wrong, I go over there a couple of times a year, and she comes over here to see me—but it still hurts sometimes, you know? And Dad—Dad is too busy being Steve Blanchard to really care about me very much. He somehow always managed to be out of the country filming or promoting a movie or something at Christmas. I actually see my mom more than I see him—and I live with him."

"That's *terrible*." I was appalled. I couldn't imagine not spending Christmas with my parents.

"Every year, I stupidly think things are going to be different, but they never are." He went on. "It's horrible to be alone at Christmas, you know? And *everything* on television is about families and the Christmas spirit. It just makes me want to slit my wrists." He sighed, "It gets to me, and I shouldn't let it, you know? That's why I called you, wanted you to come down. I hate being needy. You must think I'm the biggest dork ever."

That made me laugh. "Oh, Blair, you may be many things, but a dork? Hardly."

"Thanks for coming down," he said in a small voice.

I kissed the top of his head. "I love you, Blair. And thanks for telling me about it. You know you can tell me anything."

"I love you, Jeff." He kissed me. "You have no idea how glad I am you were daydreaming in class that day, and I decided to talk to you. You looked so cute that day. It was all I could do not to suck your dick right then and there."

"That would have been fun. You should have!"

We lay there while the sun went down, without talking, just holding each other. Around seven, though, Blair said, "We need to get in the shower. Bianca's expecting us at eight."

"Bianca?"

"I told you—Bianca del Marco has the house next door—the auteur of gay porn? She's invited us over for cocktails at eight. And we can't be late."

The shower in Blair's bathroom was amazing. The stall was large enough for about five people to fit in comfortably, and there were three nozzles, so the hot streams of water came at you from three sides. We washed each other, soaping each other up and kissing from time to time. I knew every inch of Blair's body intimately by this point—after all, there wasn't a place on his body I'd never placed my mouth—but I never got tired of touching him. Both of us got hard while we were showering, but when I started to play with his cock, he just laughed and pushed me away. "Not now, we don't have time. But I do want you to fuck me in this shower while you're here." He grinned at me. "Ever since I got here, I'd come in here and beat off, pretending you were fucking me under the water. I think it would be so much hotter in here than in the showers back at the house, don't you think?"

"Hell yeah," I said, stepping under the water to wash the soap off my body.

"You done?" Blair asked, and when I nodded, he turned the water off. We toweled each other off, and got dressed.

At promptly eight o'clock we rang the doorbell of the house next door. The door opened, and my jaw dropped. An incredibly beautiful man wearing nothing more than a gold lamé thong stood there, a big smile on his face. "Welcome to Casa del Marco," he said, kissing both of us on the cheek. "My name is Cody, and I'm here to serve you." His hair was buzzed in a military style, and one of those tribal-style tattoos circled his gigantic right bicep. His abs stood out like they'd been carved out of marble. Veins protruded from his huge muscles. And the front of the thong looked like he had—I gulped. His cock looked enormous.

Surely that couldn't be real?

Blair put his right hand directly in the center of Cody's chest, tracing down his torso with his index finger, stopping just above the top of the thong. "I'm Blair, and this is my boyfriend, Jeff."

"My pleasure," Cody replied. "Come in and join the party." He stood aside to let us pass, and it was all I could do to stop looking at him. We walked into the living room, and I couldn't take it all in. The room was crowded with beautiful young men, the music was playing loudly, and there were several other men, just as gorgeous as Cody, walking around serving drinks in the exact same thong. In a huge thronelike chair sat a huge woman who must have weighed at least three hundred pounds. She was wearing a purple dress, and her white-blond hair was teased into a gigantic bouffant that rose at least nine inches above her scalp. Her makeup was thick on her round face, and an Adam's apple showed prominently on her throat. Diamonds flashed on her fingers and dangled from her ears.

"Bianca darling!" Blair said, leaning down and kissing her large cheek. "Don't get up, dear. Thanks for the invitation."

"My pleasure." Her voice was deep and mannish. I realized with a start that Bianca was a man, I tried not to stare as she went on, "When are you going to stop being so prudish and be in one of my films?"

"Now, Bianca, you know I want to be a mainstream actor," Blair replied with a big grin, "and wonderful as your films are, it wouldn't do me any good."

"Stuff and nonsense," she replied, turning her gaze to me. A smile played over her lips, and one of her plucked eyebrows went up. "And who is this rather large and handsome boy?"

"Jeff Morgan," I said, leaning down so I wouldn't have to shout over the loud music and offering her my hand. "Blair's boyfriend."

She shook my hand. Her palm was moist and damp. "My pleasure—at least I hope so." She cackled. "Don't worry, darling, I don't bite. Unless of course you want me to? No?" She sighed. "Pity. Ah, well. You wouldn't be interested in appearing in one of my films, would you?"

"Are you serious?" I shook my head. I couldn't have heard that correctly. The music was awfully loud.

"Deadly serious. One of my performers overdosed, and had to cancel." She shook her head. Her hair didn't move. "I always say to the boys, if you can't handle your drugs, don't do them. But they never learn—they think they are indestructible." She looked at me. "Would you mind taking off your shirt for Mama?"

"Um—"

"DEVON!" she bellowed, and one of the thong-clad men came dashing over.

"Yes, Bianca?" he asked. He was naturally blond, and looked kind of like a surfer. He wasn't as muscular as Cody, but he had a beautifully shaped ass.

"Bring Mama and these two young beauties glasses of champagne, doll." He nodded and headed off to the kitchen area. "Now, don't be shy, dear. Off with your shirt!"

I looked over at Blair in a panic. He was grinning, and just nodded. I took a deep breath and pulled my T-shirt over my head. I stood there with my face turning red, holding my shirt.

Bianca whistled. "Absolutely lovely! Now, turn around."

Again, Blair nodded, so I turned around slowly in a circle. She clapped her hands together in delight. Her nails were long and painted red. "Oh, Blair, where have you been hiding this one? What a lovely body! And that ass! Blair, he's a *treasure.*" She didn't wait for him to answer as she rushed on, "Please, please help Mama out. I'll pay you fifteen hundred dollars for an afternoon's work. You can't beat that working anywhere else. All you have to do is fuck some pretty boys for the camera. Oh, you do have a big one, don't you?"

"Yes, he does," Blair said before I could say anything. My face felt hot. "And he shoots big loads, too."

I stared at him. *What are you doing to me?* I wanted to say, but then again . . . fifteen hundred dollars was a lot of money. Bianca was right. It would take me months to make that kind of money—and Dad did say I was going to have to get a job at some point . . . I could probably make fifteen hundred dollars stretch for an entire semester, if I was careful.

Devon came back with three glasses of champagne on a tray. He knelt down and Bianca took one. Blair and I took the others. I smiled my thanks at Devon, who winked and disappeared back into the crowd of people. Bianca held up her glass, and said, "To my newest star."

I looked over at Blair again. He just laughed. "Jeff, I would do it, really. There's nothing wrong with doing porn, you know."

I looked back at Bianca. I took a deep breath and leaned down and clinked my glass to hers. "I guess I'm hired then."

"Hurray! Be here tomorrow at noon." She downed her glass, and I followed suit. It was delicious; quite different than the champagne I'd chugged from the bottle at Initiation.

The rest of the party passed in a blur. I kept drinking champagne, and Bianca kept the two of us close to her. She introduced us to everyone, but after all the champagne, I was drunk and couldn't remember anyone's name. Around ten, Blair took me back to his dad's. I didn't want to leave yet, I was having a good time. But Blair insisted.

I was really drunk, and pouting. "Why did we leave? I wanted to stay."

He hadn't had as much to drink as I had, obviously. "Poor drunk little Jeffy. We left because the drugs were starting to come out. And I don't want you doing that."

"I can make my own decisions," I snapped.

"No, you can't—not when you're drunk. Now, don't get mad," he said hurriedly as I opened my mouth to snarl at him again. "First of all, you were all coked out when you slept with Marc, remember? And it wasn't coke they were going to be doing over there at Bianca's—it was crystal meth. And that's not something you want to get messed up with, my love." He sat down on my lap. "Besides, I wanted some alone time with you, is that such a bad thing?"

My anger drained out of me. "I love you, Blair. Let's go to bed."

The next morning I woke up around nine, my head aching. *Did I really agree to be in a porn movie last night?*

At noon, Blair and I rang Bianca's doorbell. This time, the door was opened by a hot little guy wearing a robe. He looked first at me, and then at Blair. "Which one of you is Jeff?"

Nervously, I swallowed. "Um, that would be me."

He looked at me, narrowing his eyes. "I'm Chad Revere. You're going to be fucking me today." He put his hands on his hips. "I guess you'll do. Just so you know, no tongues when we kiss, okay? I don't do that. I don't eat ass, either." He turned around and walked back into the house without another word.

I looked at Blair. "Great," I said, rolling my eyes. *This is off to a great start.*

Blair just laughed. "Don't be a diva on your first day on the set."

"Whatever." We walked inside. The curtains in the living room were pulled back, and there was a lot of activity around the pool. Bianca was out there, only today she was wearing a pale blue muumuu that made her look even huger than she was. She was wearing sunglasses and had a scarf wrapped around her head. A cigarette dangled from her lips. She was barking orders at a guy holding a camcorder. "That angle you shot was all wrong! We're not going to be able to use any of that footage! *Nobody* is going to pay money to see an entire fuck scene from the angle of the top's ass!"

"But, Bianca, he has a nice ass . . ."

"They pay to see penetration!" She waved her cigarette tiredly. "Oh, just go away for now and get ready for the next shot." She turned and saw me and Blair standing in the doorway. "Jeff! Blair!" She waved us to come out and join her. When we did, she lowered her sunglasses and looked at me. "All right, Jeff, are you ready for your close-up?"

My stomach was in knots. "Um, I guess," I said, hearing the trembling in my voice.

"Everyone's nervous the first time, darling, don't worry about it. Mama is here to make you look incredible, not to make you look awful. Now, get undressed."

I hesitated.

"Darling, you might as well get used to being naked in front of people."

I took off my shirt and kicked off my sandals before stripping out of my shorts and underwear. Blair took them from me, and put them in the backpack he'd brought along. Bianca smiled. "Very nice. I like the tan line. People will think you're gay for pay, and that'll sell very nicely." She sighed. "Blair, I don't understand why men like the idea of straight guys having sex with gay boys, do you?"

He shrugged. "I don't get it."

"Ah, well, it's not up to us to figure out the neuroses of our buyers."

The next hour was spent getting lighting and angles right. Chad spent the whole time either smoking or yakking on his cell phone. Bianca gave me a Viagra—"No sense in trusting you to get it up on your own the first time—most guys are camera shy the first time"—and my cock was soon totally erect. While they were setting up the shot, I posed for still photographs.

I felt like a piece of meat.

But it was also kind of exciting.

The shot called for me to come rising out of the pool stark naked. I had no lines. All I had to do was climb out of the pool and towel off, and then Chad would come out of the house and just get on his knees and start blowing me.

The irony of the shot made me grin and look over at Blair, who was trying very hard not to laugh. We were mimicking the famous scene where his father came out of the water and became a superstar.

Although by the time we were finished with it, I had a lot more sympathy for Steve Blanchard than ever before. It took half an hour and multiple takes before Bianca had one she was pleased with.

The same with the blow job sequence, and when I started fucking Chad on the chaise lounge out there. Between takes, Chad would just chain smoke and talk on his phone. I didn't know what I was expecting from him, but it wasn't that. But once the camera was on, you'd never know he was so indifferent to me. With the camera rolling, you'd think he was madly in lust with me, couldn't get enough of my cock, and just wanted me to fuck him forever. He was really good, even though I knew he was probably planning out the rest of his weekend or something in his head.

Fortunately, we got my come shot in one take.

My screen debut took just over four hours to film.

It was hard work, but I'd loved every minute of it.

It was after six o'clock when we finally made it back over to Blair's. I had to fill out reams of paperwork, have my picture taken holding up my driver's license, and then finally, just when I thought I was going to be filling out forms for the rest of my life, Bianca wrote me a check. She handed it over to me with a big smile. "You did great, kid," she said. "I definitely will use you again. I think you're going to go over real big. Do we have your contact information?"

Considering that was all on the first form I'd filled out, I nodded.

"Terrific. We'll be in touch." She waved her hand in dismissal.

Blair opened a bottle of champagne when we got back over to his father's house, and poured us both a glass. "I'm just going to order pizza, is that okay with you?"

I nodded, sipping the champagne. I was exhausted, and all I wanted to do was lie down. My butt was a little tender from being exposed to the sun for the first time ever, and my lower back ached from fucking Chad for a few hours. "I can't believe I did that."

"It's a long way from Kansas, isn't it?" he said as he dialed the number for Pizza Hut.

"Yeah."

"You okay?" he asked after he'd placed the order and hung up the phone.

"Just tired . . ."

He kissed me. "I love you."

"I love you, Blair."

But somehow, I felt like I'd changed somehow. Maybe I was just tired, but something inside of me was different. I couldn't put my finger on it, but I just felt wrong.

"I think I'm gonna take a nap," I said, standing up. "Wake me when the pizza gets here, okay?"

PART FOUR

SPRING

Chapter 12

My little brother snored and shifted on my bed.
I sat there, watching him for a minute. *He's so damned
sexy*, I thought.

I'd first met him at the New Year's Eve party.

I'd driven up from Palm Springs on December 30th, Blair
was going to come up the next day. The feeling I'd had that
day after the porn video shoot hadn't left me. I couldn't
quite figure out what was different, but something about
me was changed. I didn't know if it was from having sex on
camera, or being photographed in the nude with a hard-on,
but I didn't feel the same anymore. I wrote about it exten-
sively in my journal, trying to work my way through it, but I
never could quite put my finger on it.

I just felt like a different person. I didn't feel like Jeff
anymore.

And the worst part about it was my feelings for Blair had
changed.

I still loved him, but somehow when I looked at him I
didn't feel as intensely as I had. It was like I'd gone numb
somehow, which didn't make any kind of sense. We'd had

sex several times before we came back to Polk—in the shower, in the pool even, as well as a couple of times in the bed—and once in the living room on the marble floor under the gaze of his father's picture—but somehow things were different. It still was great sex, I still got into it, but now it was like I wasn't really a part of it. It felt sometimes like I was watching and completely detached from the whole thing. I couldn't really explain it any better than that.

I think Blair sensed it, too. He didn't say anything, but as those few days passed I noticed he wasn't as talkative as he usually was. He didn't laugh or joke as much. Instead of having fun like we always had before, the silences between us seemed to last forever, and longer.

It was like a wall had come up between us. And I didn't know how to tear it down, no matter how badly I wanted to.

So, it was kind of a relief when I got into the Flying Couch and drove back up to Polk.

I decided I was going to get royally fucked up on New Year's Eve.

It might not make things any better, but at least I wouldn't have to think about it at all. And that couldn't be a bad thing.

I bought a bag of coke from Marc Kearney, and spent the day smoking pot—I had my first bong hit in the morning after brushing my teeth. I just put a bunch of CD's in my stereo and hit shuffle, lying on the bed staring up at the ceiling. I wasn't exactly sure when Blair was going to show up, and I'd wanted to have a really good buzz going before he did. And even as I got stoned, I knew there was something wrong with us. I didn't know what it was, but the thing to do was talk it through. I wasn't being fair to Blair, I wasn't being fair to myself, but I didn't give a flying fuck about that.

So I got just really stoned.

It was around seven o'clock when Chris and Eric came by my room with a friend of theirs from high school who was thinking about going through Rush.

My first thought was *Oh my God, what a stud.*

His name was Mike Van Zale. He was only about five foot six, with light brown curly hair and freckles over his cute little snub nose. He was wearing a yellow short-sleeved pullover tucked into a tight pair of jeans, and he was muscular. Make that almost unbelievably muscular, like something out of a fitness magazine. His biceps were huge, and the shirt was pulled tight across a thick chest. "Nice to meet you," he said shyly, shaking my hand. "Chris and Eric talk about you all the time."

I opened my refrigerator and got out a can of Pepsi. I was still a little drunk from the evening's festivities. It was my first Big Brother night as a brother—and my first time getting a little brother. It'd seemed weird standing directly behind Mike, trying not to look at his muscular thick ass, and pressing a two liter bottle of Old English 800 into his hands, listening as the brothers screamed at him and the others as they stood there in their underwear trying to finish their bottles. I kept wondering *Is this what it was like for Blair last semester?* But there was a difference. Mike and I hadn't slept together, Mike and I weren't in love the way Blair and I had been. Sure, I was attracted to Mike, but I was also pretty certain that wasn't going to go anywhere. Unlike me, Mike hadn't lasted long. He'd hurried to the bathroom in the middle of Beer Relays and thrown up. Fortunately, he wasn't the first—Blair's new little brother, Jeremy Whitehead, had thrown up right after the family beer guzzling. After Mike had puked, I took pity on him and led him up to my room. He was weaving—he was a lightweight when it came to drinking. He'd been a star jock in high school, and Chris had told me that New Year's Eve was the first time he'd ever seen Mike take a drink. I was afraid that if he kept drinking, he might wind up in the emergency room, and as his big brother, it was my job to take care of him.

I knew the majority of the other brothers would force their new charges to drink again after throwing up, but I wasn't that big of an asshole. *I wonder what Blair's doing with Jeremy right now*, I thought as I made another line from the pile of cocaine on the picture of me and Blair.

Things with Blair and I had just kind of petered out after my trip to Palm Springs. We didn't talk much; I didn't go to his room and he didn't come to mine. I'd spent the entire party on New Year's Eve in my room, smoking pot, snorting coke, and drinking beer. I shared everything with Chris, Eric, and Mike. Blair never came up to my room, which didn't help my mood any that night. Especially when Chris came back after refilling a couple of pitchers from the keg and mentioned he'd run into Blair downstairs. "I told him we were up here, and told him to come on up," he said after refilling our glasses, "but he looked at me like I was insane." He shrugged. I could tell he wanted to ask me what was up, but he wouldn't in front of Mike.

Blair had driven back to Los Angeles on New Year's Day, and didn't come back until the weekend before the semester started. I didn't call him, and he didn't call me.

Sometimes when I was alone in my bed at night, I'd think about him and the distance that had sprung up between us, and wondered why it had happened. I knew it was mostly my fault, but until I knew what was wrong with me, there was nothing I could do or say to make things right between us again.

And it was soon obvious Blair didn't give a damn.

My nostrils were already numb from the coke I'd already snorted, and even though I knew doing another line wouldn't bring back the initial high from hours earlier, I still snorted it anyway. I knew all it would do was make my hands shake and make my throat rawer, my eyes sting a little bit, and gag me when the glob dripped down my throat, but I didn't care. It was a waste but I was in the stage I called the "I wants," when the high was on and I just began to mentally crave more and more cocaine. I took a hit off the bong to lessen the edge of the coke when it hit. I held the smoke in as long as I could before it exploded out of me in a massive coughing fit. I grabbed a tissue and spit out a wad of phlegm.

On the bed, Mike shifted and moaned a little.

Chris, Eric, and I had started hanging out together a lot more. I would go over to their apartment when I was horny, and we would get naked and wrestle around until we all shot a load. Coke became more and more a part of our partying, and I was burning through the fifteen hundred dollars I'd made doing the porn movie pretty damned quickly.

I was out of control and I didn't know why.

I took a sip of the soda to cool my burning throat and walked over to the bed. Mike was sprawled on his back on top of the covers. In the moonlight coming through the slightly parted curtains, his skin looked like smooth alabaster. His hairless and hard chest gleamed in the ghostly light. Thick wiry hair sprouted from under his arms. A thin line of drool hung from the corner of his mouth. His face was expressionless. A thin trail of wiry black hairs ran from his navel to the waistband of his white briefs.

He was quite beautiful.

Looking at him, I felt my dick getting hard. I'd started beating off to fantasies about Mike right after I saw him shirtless for the first time. His upper body was amazing, but Chris and Eric had warned me at the New Year's party that he wasn't like us. "He's a straight boy, through and through," Eric had said. "If he isn't, he's completely oblivious. We've hinted to him any number of times, but nothing's ever happened. So be careful."

He'd spilled beer on his shirt at the end of rush party, and I'd offered to loan him one. He came up to my room and pulled his shirt over his head and I'd caught my breath.

"Thanks," he'd said as he pulled my sweater over his head. "I'll wash it before I give it back, okay?"

And now he was my little brother.

I knew I was playing with fire.

Looking down at his chest, I thought, *I should have said no.*

But you took a little brother because Blair took a new one, replacing you.

Jeremy Whiteside was a nice guy, too, but he did nothing for me physically. I didn't know if he and Blair were fucking, but it didn't really matter to me one way or the other. Blair and I were finished.

I started to make another line of coke, but stopped myself.

I looked over at Mike.

You shouldn't have taken him as your little brother because you want him.

Mike had attached himself to me after I loaned him the sweater. During Rush, I had taken him around and introduced him to the other brothers. Mike's effect on the little sisters was almost painfully obvious, but Mike seemed unaware of the looks he was getting from the girls, remaining focused almost entirely on me and everything I said. He'd accepted a pledge bid that night, and on his daily visits to the house he always stopped by my room first. As the weeks passed leading up to the selection of Big Brothers, I knew that Mike was going to pick me. I also knew that Mike had slept with some of the little sisters after parties, and the girls, who for whatever reason always seemed to confide in me, had told me that Mike had "a big one." Jennifer West, a senior who'd been around since she was a freshman, told me "He's as big as Rory, if you can believe that."

And now there it was, covered only by a thin layer of white cotton, just inches from me.

I want you, I whimpered out loud, and then laughed at myself. I could hear Bianca's voice in my head, asking *why do gay men always fall in love with straight boys? Why is that such a turn on for us?*

Why, indeed.

Maybe because they're unattainable.

How many times had I dreamed about him, fantasized about him while I masturbated, picturing us lying in bed together naked, kissing, nibbling on Mike's big nipples, trailing my tongue down the flat stomach. I could feel Mike's big strong arms around me, pulling me in closer and more tightly as our lips met, Mike's full sensual lips parting and my tongue sliding into Mike's mouth, feeling his slightly crooked front teeth with my tongue. Mike's beautiful slate-blue eyes slightly closed in pleasure as he slowly began to grind his crotch against mine, our erections straining against each other longing for release.

I reached my trembling hand out towards Mike, pausing just above his half-dollar-sized right nipple. Mike's even breathing raised his chest almost to where it would touch my hand and then dropped back down. *How does your skin feel*, I wondered, *is it cool and smooth and velvety or hot and fevered?*

As though in answer, Mike moaned a little in his sleep.

Reflexively, my hand shot back, and I reached for the bong again. I lit the bowl, inhaling gently until the water began to bubble, and the cool smoke snaked its way up the long glass neck and entered my mouth and into my lungs. I put the bong back on the desk and held the breath as long as I could before expelling it toward the ceiling, a fog of curls.

Mike shifted again in his sleep, muttering incomprehensible sounds, the gibberish of the sleeping. My left hand slid up from the bedspread and rested on my lower abdomen, just above the elastic waistband of my underwear.

I looked at the hand as the smoke began to do its magic on my mind. Mike's hand was beautifully shaped, big and strong with black hairs curling along the side of it just below the pinkie. His fingers were strong rather than stubby and meaty, graceful, an artist's hand.

Yeah, right, an artist's hand, my voice mocked inside my head. *He has the IQ of a doorknob. He doesn't get the jokes on "ALF", for God's sake. His favorite movie is "Rambo". He has never read a book he didn't have to for class. He has the body of a god and the soul of a, well, face it, the soul of a peasant.*

But he's so incredibly sweet, not a mean bone in his body, I amended. Never mean-spirited. He was sweet and gentle

and kind, with never a bad word for anyone or about anything.

Almost childlike in his simplicity.

I reached out again toward the nipple, the mound of
muscle lying on the rib cage. I wanted to touch his nipple,
tweak it softly, pull on it a little bit, just to see what would
happen, to see if he would wake.

What if he did wake to me hovering over his near-naked
body? To having his nipple toyed with?

His eyes could open slowly with a slow moan, "That
feels good, Jeff, I like that." And he would give me that lazy
smile, the one that exposed the slightly crooked teeth, and
take me by the hand and pull me onto the bed with him,
using my free hand to release his huge cock from the white
cotton restraints, and we would kiss as I fumbled out of my
clothes until we were both naked on the coverlet, Mike
rolling me over until I was on my back, my legs going up in
the air as Mike spit on his hands and wet his cock, then sliding it into me, and I would open for its intrusion, its pleasure bringing hardness sliding deep inside of me until I had
to clench my teeth to keep from screaming, it felt so
damned good, and Mike would gently rock his hips back
and forth, teasing me, taunting me as he slowly slid out before plunging deeply back in, my breath coming in gasps
until I could hold myself back no longer and shot a long
stringy rope of come out, raindrops of white falling on my
chest and stomach as Mike smiled down at me before
pulling out and finishing himself off as well.

And then Mike would move in with me, in my very
room. We would put in another bed for appearance's sake,
but every night we would slowly undress each other before
climbing into bed, kissing and caressing and loving each

other, before making love and then go to sleep, and in the mornings we would wake in each other's arms, loving each other, happy and contented. We would both graduate from college and move down to LA, get a great place in the Hollywood hills, with a pool and a hot tub, and invitations to parties at the Morgan-Van Zale's would be the most sought after, the most prestigious in the West Hollywood scene. Other men, models, actors, producers, agents, directors, would try to steal Mike away from me by offering to make him a star, by offering him cars and jewelry and money, and Mike would always just smile and say, "Thank you, but no, I am in love with Jeff and can't live without him in my life." And we would grow old together, a permanent fixture in the West Hollywood social scene, me writing my books and Mike doing, well, whatever it was he wanted to do. And every night, we would share a glass of red wine before making love and going to sleep, celebrating our life together.

Our love.

I smiled. It could happen that way, I thought to myself. Yeah, sure it could.

Or Mike could open his eyes. "What the hell are you doing?" he would say, shaking his head, trying to clear it from the raging hangover and the overwhelming sense that something was wrong, something was terribly, terribly wrong.

"I, uh. I . . ." I would panic, the cocaine and the pot and the alcohol rushing together in my clouded head as I tried to think of a plausible reason why I had been tugging on Mike's nipple, why I still was! I would pull my hand back as if burned.

Mike would sit up, awareness dawning on his face. "You're a fag," he would say, his beautiful eyes narrowing in disgust and hatred, his lips curling back over the crooked teeth in a sneer. "A fucking faggot! Were you going to suck my dick next?" And then aware that he was only in his underwear, he would shove me back and away, with me falling backwards, hitting the wall with a thump loud enough to wake everyone else in the house as Mike grabbed for his pants and pulled them on, his voice rising as he continued to rant. "A fucking fag! Beta Kappa, some fucking fraternity! Are you all butt brothers? Is that what this place is? A fucking faggot recruitment center?"

Voices in the hall, pounding on the door, Mike pulling his sweater over his head.

"Mike, please—" I would beg from the floor, unable to move, unable to do anything as Mike opened the door and other fraternity brothers came into the room, and told them what I had been doing, and my carefully protected life, the one of acceptance and fraternity and friendship that I had worked so long and so hard to build, would be gone as Mike screamed at them that Jeff was a fag, Jeff was a fag, Jeff was a fag.

"He's lying . . ." I would try to say, but the words clogged in my throat, wouldn't come out, and then my brothers were turning to look at me, and my best friend, my closest friends, Chris and Eric would have to play along, their faces twisted with loathing and hatred and contempt as they spat the word out, "Fag."

I finished the soda and stood up. I looked down at Mike and then peered through the curtains. The sun was coming up.

I reached out and shook Mike's shoulder. "Mike."

Mike's eyes opened and his mouth worked slowly. "Jeff? What the—"

"I let you sleep in my room, but it's time for you to get

back home." I smiled as I spoke the words slowly, softly, gently. "The worst thing in the world is for a pledge to be in the house the morning after Big Brother Night." I bent down and picked up Mike's clothes from the floor and handed them to him.

Mike stood up and rubbed his eyes. "I feel like shit."

"Go on home and get some sleep."

Mike yawned and stretched, muscles flexing and contracting all over his body. I turned my head.

I couldn't watch, not anymore.

Mike pulled his clothes on in an agony of movement, tied his shoes and gave me a hug. "Thanks for watching out for me."

"What are big brothers for? Come on by tonight and I'll take you out for a nice dinner."

Mike smiled. "Thanks, Jeff."

The door closed behind him. I got another soda and walked over to the window. I stood there until Mike came out the door, and watched him walk away down the sidewalk. My right hand made a fist, and I gently pounded the window with it twice as he watched.

Then, I undressed. I slid beneath the sheets. I could smell Mike's presence there, and the sheets were still warm from Mike's body.

I'm tired of not being who I am, I thought. *I'm tired of hiding who I am from everyone.*

With a rush of sudden clarity, everything became plain to me.

I walked back over to my desk and sat down hard, reaching for my bong.

That was what went wrong for me in Palm Springs.

I heard Blair saying again to Bianca that he couldn't do

the movie because it might affect his future career as an actor. I thought back to that night, to that party. *Why had I agreed to make the movie? It wasn't just the money, even though that was what I told myself that night. It was really because I was going to be recorded on film having sex with another man—there was going to be a public record that I was a gay man. Anyone who wanted, from that moment on, to find out that I was gay could do so if they tried hard enough, if they knew where to look. And that's what changed things with Blair. Making that movie was freeing for me. I felt like I was finally showing the world who I was . . . and after it was over I went back next door with Blair and back to our hidden relationship. We loved each other, but we were keeping it a secret.*

And that was why things had changed between us, that was why I didn't care so much anymore.

I was in love with him, and he with me, but we were in hiding.

My entire life was a lie.

The only time I ever felt like I was being honest was when I was doing that stupid movie.

Beta Kappa had meant everything to me when I'd been going through my pledge semester. I'd wanted so desperately to join, to belong. Part of it was Blair, but with only a few exceptions, I'd liked the brothers and wanted to be a part of the house.

The notion that they would hate me if they knew the truth about me, that they would throw me out on my ass, turn their backs on me and drum me out of the Brotherhood if they knew was against everything about Beta Kappa that I'd loved and wanted to be a part of.

Chapter 13

"**A**re you completely insane?" Blair stared at me. He was wearing a pair of red sweatpants and a white tank top, sitting at his desk with his laptop open. I was sitting on his bed, taking a hit out of the dragon. He shook his head. "I mean, really, Jeff, what is wrong with you?" He shook his head. "What purpose would it serve?"

I blew out the smoke. "There's nothing wrong with me at all." I coughed for a few minutes—the pot was really harsh—and wiped the tears out of my eyes. "For the first time in a long time, I'm right, if you know what I mean." I handed the dragon back to him. "I just can't keep hiding who I am. It's wrong." *And I am not going to do it anymore*, I added to myself.

Blair just sat there, staring at me with his mouth open. It was the Sunday after Big Brother Night. It had taken me two days to steal my nerve to come down and talk to him. I'd rehearsed what I was going to say over and over again, trying to think of a calm, rational way to convince him that I was right, to get him to realize that it was the right thing to do. I'd avoided the other brothers, staying in my room and studying, working on a story for my fiction writing class, but I couldn't stay focused. Different options kept coming to me. *What if Blair says no, you can't convince him, are you willing to stand alone in front of the brotherhood and be honest? How am I going to tell Mom and Dad?* But I couldn't do anything without talking to him, without trying to make things right between the two of us. I loved him, and I wasn't sure that would ever change. I missed him. I wanted to be with him again. He'd changed my life, helped me to face up to who I really was, and I owed him. I missed the feel of his body against mine, his kisses, those wonderful moments after we had both just came and lay there, panting and sweating in each other's arms. If there was no future for us, so be it—but I had to make the attempt.

What will you do if he refuses to come out to the brothers? How can you be together then?

I figured I'd cross that bridge when I came to it.

My hands were sweating as I walked down to his room, going over what I planned to say to him one more time.

Of course, once I finally knocked on the door and was in his room, I'd just blurted it out. *Blair, I think we need to come out to the Brotherhood.*

"I admire you for your courage, Jeff," he finally said. "If you think you need to, for yourself, that's fine. But it's not something I'm ready to do." His hands shook slightly as he took a hit off the dragon. "I don't know if I'll ever be able to." His eyes looked a little wet. "I just don't know."

"Aren't you tired of lying?" I asked, my heart sinking. I felt like crying myself. I knew I wasn't going to be able to convince him. "Aren't you tired of pretending to be something you aren't? We're not supposed to lie to the brothers, you know." I pleaded with him. "Remember? 'A brother never lies to another brother.' It was one of our pledge lessons."

"Exactly." Blair put the bong down on his desk. "They won't drum us out of the Brotherhood for being gay, Jeff. They'll drum us out for lying about it. We've committed an honor code violation, and that's what they'll use to throw us out."

I opened my mouth, and then closed it again. I couldn't think of anything else to say to him.

"The ideals of the Brotherhood, Jeff, are just that— ideals. Something to strive for." He shook his head again. "But ideals aren't reality, and you know that—deep down, you know it. Not all of the brothers are that open-minded, you know. Some of them wouldn't care about us being gay, but more of them then you think would . . . and they'd use the lying to throw us right out of here." He gave a hollow laugh. "They would have never pledged either one of us if they'd known—but then they'll drum us out for not telling."

"I don't believe that," I replied stubbornly. "And besides, if that's the case, they aren't maybe the kind of brothers I'd want to have anyway."

"So, Jeff, are you willing to risk the Brotherhood for this?" he asked. "Because that's the bottom line. You could lose everything you have here."

"If it's based on a lie, Blair, what exactly do I have here?" I sighed. "Blair, I just—fuck, I don't know."

"I've missed you," he went on, reaching over and placing his hand on my knee. "I knew something changed for you in Palm Springs, and so I gave you your space, thinking you just needed some time, and you'd get over whatever it was that was bothering you, and you'd come back to me. It killed me, you know." He swallowed, and wiped tears out of his eyes. "It killed me knowing you were just upstairs and I couldn't be with you." He sighed, "And this is what it was all about, right?"

I nodded, and placed my own hand over his, squeezing it. "Blair, I—I've always loved you. That's not ever going to stop."

Blair started laughing.. "God, I am such a *fucking* drama queen. I thought you were pissed about doing the movie, and you blamed me for getting you into it. And I was so pissed at myself, you know, for risking what we had by—"

I rolled my eyes and started laughing. "No, I'm GLAD I made the movie—it was making the movie that started all this—it was while making the movie I felt free, and then when we went back to your dad's, it was like I was, I don't know. It just didn't feel right anymore to keep everything a secret. I mean, I knew something in me had changed—and it wasn't a bad thing, Blair, you have to believe that. But to be honest, I didn't even figure it out myself until the other night, when Mike was passed out in my bed." I rubbed my eyes. "I just feel like a fraud, Blair. I mean, how can I teach Mike about what it means to be a brother when I'm not a good brother? And I had to ask myself, would Mike have chosen me as his big brother had he known the truth? I can't keep this up. It's driving me crazy."

"You take this stuff too seriously." Blair answered. "Don't get me wrong, I think it's great—maybe it's the creative writer in you, I don't know. But you need to stop worrying about this kind of stuff. It's stuff you can't control. Like I said before, the brotherhood has wonderful ideals, but what you need to understand is that ideals are something to strive for, and they're not necessarily reality." He reloaded the bong. "People aren't perfect—not that any of us ever claimed to be, God knows I'm not, but we need ideals so that we can try to be better people."

"Yeah, but—"

"No buts." He cut me off. "The Brotherhood is only as strong as its weakest link, remember that? There are plenty of weak links around here. And don't think brothers don't suspect about you and me. There's been plenty of talk around here about us, don't ever think there isn't. Or wasn't, I don't know if there still is or not. And nobody cared, Jeff, that's the important thing. They didn't care enough to say anything to either of us, to keep you from being initiated, or to bring us up in front of the Brotherhood."

"So, as long as we keep it quiet, everything will be okay?"

"They don't care as long as we don't make an issue of it. We make an issue of it, they'll drum us out on honor code. Period."

I sighed. "I suppose." I stood up. "I'm glad we talked."

"So am I." he looked over at me. "You want to come down later and—um." He hesitated.

"I can think of nothing I would rather do." I walked over and kissed the top of his head. "I've missed you, too."

"Are we good now?"

I nodded.

"You don't have to go, if you don't want to." He cleared his throat. "I'd like it if you stayed . . ."

I got up and walked over to where he was sitting, and knelt down in between his legs. I leaned into him and pressed my mouth against his, and he let out that low moan I'd missed hearing from down in his throat. I slid my tongue into his mouth and he started sucking on it as his hands went down and undid my jeans. He slid a hand inside my pants and started gently rubbing the head of my cock. I slid my mouth down to his right nipple and started teasing it with my lips and my tongue, and his head went back. With my righ hand I grabbed hold of his hard-on through his sweat pants.

"Oh, God, Jeff, I've missed you so much . . ." he whispered. He pushed me away, and stood up, sliding his sweatpants down and stepping out of them. I smiled and pulled my shirt up over my head. Immediately he put his mouth on my nipples as I slid my pants down, and began nibbling first on the right one, before moving over to the left. My cock was ready to explode. He pushed me back down on the bed and took my cock in his mouth, sliding his mouth up and down on me. It felt so amazing. I just tilted my head back and gave in to the sensation of his warm wet mouth on my cock. He nibbled on the head a bit, teasing it with his teeth and then licking it until I thought I was going to explode. My entire body began to arch up—and then he put his hands on my stomach and smiled at me. "Oh no, not yet, my love." He slid a condom on over me, straddling me. I reached up and started playing with his nipples. His breath started coming in gasps as he lowered himself down on me, and began riding me.

I'd missed being inside him. I'd almost forgotten what it felt like to have my cock in his ass, and I started bucking my hips up. I loved him so much, I wanted us to be joined, I wanted my cock to go as far inside of him as I could get it. I always felt so much closer to him when we were fucking . . . and he was smiling at me until his eyes closed in pleasure and the moans started coming from deep inside his chest.

After we both came, he lay down beside me on the bed, our arms around each other. I could hear him breathing, could hear his heartbeat, and it was almost as though our hearts were beating in sync with one another.

This is love, and there's no way this could be wrong, I told myself before I finally closed my eyes and went to sleep.

So, we patched up our problems and fell back into our old routine—spending a lot of time together, furtively making love whenever we got the chance.

And what he said finally started making some sense to me. I went over to my parents' house a couple of times for dinner, steeling myself on the drive over to have The Talk, and found that when I was looking at them across the dinner table I couldn't do it. *There's a lot you don't know about being gay,* I thought to myself one night as I headed back to the house after chickening out again, *and outside of Blair, you really don't have anyone you can talk to about it.* Obviously, I couldn't join the Gay Student Group on campus—maybe after I outed myself to the Brotherhood, but surely not until then. So, I made up a new email address, and started posting questions about being gay on groups all over the Internet. I wanted to know what other people thought about the situation I found myself in, and wasn't prepared for the responses I got to my posts.

Some were angry:

By staying in the closet, you're telling your fraternity brothers they're right to discriminate against other gay people and it's okay to be homophobic. By staying in the closet and not being yourself you're harming other openly gay college students. People like your fraternity brothers think it's okay to hate gay people because they think they don't know any—but they really do.

Are you proud of yourself? Does it feel good to live a lie? Why would you want to be friends with people who wouldn't like you if they knew who you really were?

And others were supportive:

Don't listen to people who want to insult you or berate you for living your life the way you chose to. They don't know what your life is like or anything about who you are or what you're going through unless they've been in the same exact situation. Coming out of the closet is difficult for anyone, no matter who they are, and it sounds to me like you're getting to the point where you are going to be ready to—but you aren't there yet, otherwise you wouldn't be questioning the decision. When you're ready, it will feel right and you will know it. Don't be bullied into something you aren't ready for yet.

Hang in there!

It wasn't much help, frankly.

So I pretty much just focused on studying, spending time with Blair, and being a good big brother to Mike. I still was incredibly attracted to him—who wouldn't be? But it was pretty apparent that Mike was a straight boy, and not one of those who was a little on the frisky side after a six pack or so. I also didn't feel right about trying to take advantage of him when he was drunk—he was such a sweet guy. He never had anything bad to say about anyone, and even when he was hanging out with me and Blair, smoking pot and drinking beer, and we'd say shit about other brothers, he could always find something nice to say about them. And after he would go back to his apartment, Blair would just look at me and say, "He's almost too nice to be real, isn't he?"

I would just laugh, and then we'd start kissing, and forget all about him.

Life was good, I guess, but I still wasn't comfortable lying to the Brotherhood.

But I was pretty sure the right time would come.

* * *

The semester seemed to fly by, much quicker than I would have ever thought possible. Blair wanted me to come spend the summer with him in Los Angeles—his father was going to be in southeast Asia somewhere making a movie, and his mother was doing a play in London. "I am not spending the summer in London," he said after he got off the phone with her. He gave me a crooked grin. "I am not going all summer without seeing you."

He got a big kiss for that.

And I felt a lot better about everything. My grades were high, I actually liked my classes—especially my Fiction Writing class, and for Spring Break, Blair and I planned on going down to Palm Springs to stay at his dad's again. "I'm not making another movie," I said with a laugh when he first suggested the trip.

"As if I would let you!" He grinned back at me. "I'm not going to go through that again."

On the Friday morning before spring break started, there was a knock on my door. "It's open!" I called out from my desk. I was trying to finish writing a short story that was due to my creative writing class the Monday after spring break. I wanted to have it finished so I wouldn't have to worry about it over the break. I looked up. "Oh, hey, Marc."

Marc Kearney came in and shut the door behind. "Are you busy?"

I had maybe another five hundred words to add to the story, but that probably wouldn't take a lot of time to do. "Nothing that can't keep for a bit. What's going on?"

He bit his lip. "I don't know how to say this, Jeff, so I am going to come right out and say it. You've been reported to the Executive Council for an honor code violation."

My entire body went cold. "What? Why? What did I do?"

"Look, I'm not supposed to be telling you any of this, okay? But the Executive Council met last night, and when break is over, they're going to call you in on Monday afternoon to determine whether or not to put you on trial before the entire Brotherhood."

"What am I supposed to have done?" *Someone knows* raced through my head, followed just as quickly by *I knew I should have gone before the Brotherhood when I wanted to.*

"I'm telling you all of this because I like you and think you have a lot to offer to the house." Marc went on like I hadn't said anything. "A lot more than Ted Norris, that's for goddamned sure. I can't believe he would do this to you after what happened during Inspiration Week—you'd think the little fuck would be grateful, but no! And just how he found out about you in the first place is what I would like to know. So, I think you should be prepared—it's only fair."

"Marc, I appreciate this." I felt lightheaded. "But what have I done?"

"There's a movie being advertised on the Internet, *Pool Studs,* or something like that. Anyway, there's a guy in this movie who looks just like you. They have lots of pictures of him on their website, and Ted showed it to the Executive Council." Marc patted my shoulder. "I'm sure it's just a coincidence—"

I started laughing. "No, it's no coincidence, Marc. No coincidence at all. It's me. I made that movie while I was in Palm Springs during winter break."

"Oh." He bit his lip, and I couldn't help wondering if he was thinking about that night during Little Sister Rush when I was a pledge. "You can always deny it, you know, stranger things have happened, you can just say the guy looks like you—"

"I have no intention of denying it, Marc." The initial panic was over, and I knew then that I was never going to deny who I was anymore. I felt remarkably calm. The decision had been made for me, and that was my only regret—I just wished I had been the one to decide when to tell the Brotherhood the truth. And of all people, to have Ted Norris be the one to out me to the Brotherhood. There was a kind of delicious irony there. Ted thought he was punishing me for some reason—getting even for slights during our pledge semester. I wasn't even angry at him. It was kind of funny in a way.

If he only knew he was doing me a favor! That was certainly going to take all the pleasure out of it for him, wasn't it?

"Are you sure you want to do that?"

"Marc, don't worry. I'm not going to expose you or what happened between us. That's between you and your conscience. But I'm not going to be another Ted and betray anyone else to the Executive Council." I folded my arms. "Unlike Ted, I believe in the ideals of the Brotherhood."

He reached out and shook my hand. "For what's worth, I won't vote to blackball you."

"Thanks, Marc."

I sat there staring at my computer screen for a while, and after a few minutes, I started laughing. Poor stupid Ted! He was probably all proud of himself—thinking he was bringing me down once and for all. He was in for a big surprise after spring break. The only question was *how is Blair going to handle this?*

The only thing I had, the only thing that was fair, was to be completely honest with him.

I told Blair on the drive down to Palm Springs.

"That miserable little son of a bitch!" Blair swore. "I'll kill him!"

"You don't need to, I'm actually glad this is all coming out, Blair," I replied. "Keep your eyes on the road! No, there isn't going to be a trial before the Brotherhood, Blair. When we get back, I am going before the Executive Council, tell them the truth, and resign from the house. I'm not going to fight this, I'm not going to lie about it, I'm not going to keep hiding who and what I am. And after I resign from the Brotherhood, I'm going to go tell my parents. And don't worry, I'm not going to out you to the Executive Council."

He was silent. After a few moments, he said, "You won't have to. I'm going in with you and resign as well."

My heart swelled with love and pride. "You don't have to—"

"I know I don't have to, Jeff. I *want* to." He laughed. "Who wants to be a part of a house that would throw you out and keep fucking Ted Norris?"

"Please don't use the word *fucking* in conjunction with Ted Norris." I shuddered. "That's a mental image I don't want to have."

We both laughed, and that was the end of the discussion.

Spring Break was absolutely amazing. Blair and I had a blast, partying and meeting other out college kids. We had the most amazing sex, as well as our first three way with a hot guy from UCLA who belonged to a gay fraternity there. But even as each day passed, and the day of reckoning drew nearer, I felt freer. I was looking forward to that Monday, and it couldn't come fast enough for me.

And Monday afternoon, Blair and I walked into the President's office to meet with the Executive Council, holding hands. They all stared at us.

"Esteemed brothers," I said. "Brother Blanchard and I wish to request permission to address the Executive Council."

"Permission granted," Jake Beardsley, the current President, stated. He was still staring at our linked hands. He looked a little pale. I'd always liked Jake, even though I'd never really gotten to know him all that well.

I cleared my throat. "I am offering my resignation from the Brotherhood. I have violated the honor code of Beta Kappa by lying to the brotherhood. I have been lying to the brotherhood ever since I first accepted my pledge bid. I have never once outright told a lie, or answered a question with a lie, but rather have lied by not being honest about myself to the Brotherhood. I am a gay man. I am in love with Brother Blanchard, and we have been in a relationship since last summer, before I accepted my pledge bid. As such, I have no recourse other than to resign from the Brotherhood."

Jake's face went even paler, and his eyes bulged a bit. "Is this true, Brother Blanchard?" He managed to choke out, and I wondered what he had thought when Ted had come to them with his accusation.

"Yes, Brother Beardsley, it is true," Blair answered. "I too am offering my resignation."

"It saddens me to hear this," Jake cleared his throat, and looked around at the other members of the Council before continuing. "I don't think these honor violations require either of you to resign from the Brotherhood. I understand why the two of you might have felt the need to deceive the

Brotherhood, and I can assure you that on my part, there was no need. My older brother is a gay man as well—and I feel that both of you are an asset to the house, assets that will be sorely missed. I move that we do not accept your resignations and rather put it to a vote by the entire Brotherhood at our meeting this evening."

"I second that," Marc said.

"Are there any objections?" When no one said a word, Jake said, "We will put it the Brotherhood tonight. You two are excused."

Back in Blair's room, we sat down together on the bed. "What do you think will happen tonight?" I asked. "It sounded to me like they'd already talked about it a lot—but they didn't expect us to come in there and be honest and admit to it. And in a way, it's kind of passing the buck by sending it to the whole Brotherhood in a way . . . but then again, I guess—oh, I don't know." I took his hand. "No, it couldn't be decided by them. I *want* the entire Brotherhood to vote on it. I don't want anyone saying later they didn't have a say in it."

Blair shrugged. " Maybe, Jeff." He leaned over and kissed me. "All I know is regardless of how it all comes out, we don't have to hide our love from anyone ever again." And he put his head down on my chest. "And that's the best thing. You were right, Jeff. I feel so *relieved.*"

Without question, it was the longest afternoon I'd ever spent in my life. We stayed in Blair's room until we were sent for by the Brotherhood. When the knock on the door finally came, Marc Kearney's face was solemn. "The Brotherhood is ready for you, now."

We followed him into the Great Room, where the brothers were all seated at the dining tables formed into a large circle. We were led into the center of the circle, and faced the Executive Council. I stole a quick glance around the solemn faces of the Brotherhood, and noticed that Ted wasn't one of them.

"Ted's not here." I whispered to Blair.

Jake cleared his throat. "Brothers Blanchard and Morgan, the Brotherhood has voted on your application to resign from Beta Kappa fraternity." He paused, and I could feel the sweat forming under my arms. "There was much vigorous discussion. But ultimately, the Brotherhood decided that the two of you did violate the honor code." My heart sank. "But the Brotherhood also decided that there were extenuating circumstances that led to this violation, and it is not the Brotherhood's intent to be unjust or unfair. So the Brotherhood has rejected your resignations. You are both, however, placed on a two semester probation for the violation. Another violation, and your membership will be revoked." He slammed his gavel down on the table. "May this matter be closed forever."

I stood there for a moment, not believing what I'd just heard.

And then, every single one of the brothers cheered.

Before we knew it, our brothers had surrounded us, clapping and hugging us.

"Meeting is dismissed!" Jake shouted over the noise.

"Just don't be looking at me in the shower," Jerry Pollard said as he hugged me.

"Don't worry," I teased him back and we both laughed.

When Marc Kearney hugged me, I whispered to him, "Where's Ted?"

"Ted resigned." Marc said with a sigh. "It was—I can't describe it, Jeff. When the vote went in your favor, he tore off his pin, announced he wouldn't be a part of a Brotherhood that would condone such immoral behavior, and stormed out." He shrugged. "Good riddance to bad rubbish, I say."

"Immoral behavior?" I started laughing. "He said that? Has he ever been to a party at this place?"

Marc cracked up.

Finally, Blair and I made it back to his room, joined by a group of brothers. We smoked pot, drank, and laughed and sang the fraternity song.

And finally, around midnight, we were alone together.

"We did it," Blair said, unbuttoning my shirt.

"There's nothing we can't do as long as we do it together." I leaned down and kissed him on the mouth.

"I love you, Jeff."

"I love you, Blair."

And that night, we went to sleep in each others' arms in his bed with the curtains wide open, so anyone who walked by could see us.

We were never going to have to hide ever again.

Just before I fell asleep, I looked over at Blair's closet. I could see a red sweatshirt with the big black and white BK on the front.

Beta Kappa.

Tears of joy filled my eyes, and then I laughed.

I sure have come a long way from Kansas.

And what a great journey it's been.